Gillian Kaye is the author of several novels. She lives in Pickering, North Yorkshire.

# A DARING DISGUISE

At the outbreak of the French Revolution, the de Charnay family escape from Paris to their Welford cousins in Sussex. However, several complications arise. First, Marianne Welford quarrels with her fiancé, Harvey Burrage-Smith MP, when he refuses to go to help her French cousins; then, when the de Charnays arrive, there is an immediate attraction between Marianne's sister Lucy and Edouard de Charnay — an attraction not easily resolved. As the tension rises, Marianne and Harvey travel to Paris admidst turmoil and conflict, but there must be many adventures before the two families can finally settle down to their new lives.

*Books by Gillian Kaye*
*Published by The House of Ulverscroft:*

WAITING FOR MATT
HEARTBREAK AT HAVERSHAM
CONFLICT OF HEARTS
MYSTERY AT MELBECK
A LOVE BEYOND REACH
ISLAND FOR FIONA
TO LOVE IN VAIN
FORBIDDEN LOVE
SO TANGLED A WEB

GILLIAN KAYE

# A DARING DISGUISE

*Complete and Unabridged*

# ULVERSCROFT
*Leicester*

First published in Great Britain in 2004 by
Robert Hale Limited
London


First Large Print Edition
published 2005
by arrangement with
Robert Hale Limited
London

The moral right of the author has been asserted

British Library CIP Data

Kaye, Gillian
    A daring disguise.—Large print ed.—
    Ulverscroft large print series: romantic suspense
    1. France—History—Revolution, 1789 – 1799—Fiction
    2. Love stories 3. Large type books
    I. Title
    823.9′14 [F]

    ISBN 1–84395–559–8

Published by
F. A. Thorpe (Publishing)
Anstey, Leicestershire

Set by Words & Graphics Ltd.
Anstey, Leicestershire
Printed and bound in Great Britain by
T. J. International Ltd., Padstow, Cornwall

This book is printed on acid-free paper

# 1

Paris 1793. A city of blood, of death, of the Terror. A city of the Revolution.

To Annette de Charnay, young daughter of Maurice de Charnay, Comte St Amand, a city of fear. She sat quietly enough in the salon of the Maison Charnay at Auteuil on the outskirts of Paris; the stillness of her pale face did not reveal any of the turmoil of her emotions.

It was 18 October, the mornings were crisp and cold, the evenings becoming dark; the leaves on the trees in the parkland behind the de Charnay house were turning to gold and beginning to scatter their rich colours over the grass.

Two days before, Queen Marie Antoinette had gone to the guillotine and the citizens of Paris either rejoiced or trembled. The working people of St Antoine joined the mob at the Place de la Grève, they crowded the windows of the tall houses, they hung on to the rooftops. They screamed in a frenzy or they sat implacably around the Place, women too old to climb to the roof-tops who sat and knitted their way through the events of those awful days. They were known as the *tricoteuses* and as they knitted, they counted the heads falling into the basket at the foot of the guillotine.

Those in Paris who trembled that day of 16 October were such as the de Charnays, the aristocratic families, the hated Royalists. Many had already perished at the hand of Robespierre and the Committee of Public Safety, many had succeeded in escaping to Austria and to England.

The fact that Maurice de Charnay, Comte d'Amand, had married an English girl, Caroline Vilven; the fact that he had treated all who worked on his estates with great generosity and thoughtfulness, counted for nothing. The comte and his family knew that their turn would come and they had made their plans.

To attempt to drive from Paris in their own carriage would mean certain capture and death; the comte knew this and he had sent a message to his wife's family in Sussex to ask for their assistance.

While they awaited their fate, each one of the small family of four lay hidden or disguised; Annette de Charnay, fifteen years of age, played the most difficult part of all.

As soon as the death of the queen became known, Monsieur le Comte and his wife and children — Edouard, the Vicomte, and Annette — gathered in the kitchen of the big house, together with Mme Marais, their cook of twenty years. No fires had been lit in the other rooms and the kitchen was the warmest place in the house. The five of them sat round the long, wooden table scrubbed almost white with years of use; cook had made mugs of coffee and with the heat of the old-fashioned, wood-burning range, they were comfortable in body if not in spirit.

The count was a tall and serious man; black hair with hints of grey, and dark eyes in a long face, once handsome but now etched with lines of worry and care.

'Caroline, my dear children,' he said gravely. 'We have heard the sound of tumbrels on the road for many months, and since King Louis died in January, we have known that our turn would come. We have hidden in the woods many times, but our lives have been spared. I have no need to tell you that each day, the Terror gets worse. The mob howls for blood and now our queen has been taken from us. There is no news from England, but we must be prepared to be ready if our cousins come for us.'

He looked around him; at his wife, only a few years younger than himself, still with her glorious fair hair and beautiful in her calm composure. He could rely on Caroline, she would do whatever he asked of her and do it bravely.

Then there were his two children. Strange, he thought, they had wanted a large, jolly family, but now he must give thanks that he had only Edouard and Annette to consider.

Edouard, his son and heir, as tall as himself, but young and handsome. Edouard had inherited the dark hair of the de Charnays, but he had his mothers blue-grey eyes, a striking contrast. He was twenty years of age and his studies at the university had been interrupted.

But his little Annette; the count still thought of her as little even though her sixteenth birthday was near. She sat with her hand in her mother's and was composed. Not pretty, the comte thought, her hair was a very ordinary brown and her face did not bear the distinguished lines of the de Charnays. But like Edouard, she had her mother's eyes and at that moment, they were steady and brave. He was glad of this for he was going to ask her to do something which required both courage and resourcefulness.

Edouard broke into his father's thoughts. 'What is it that you require of us, Papa?'

The comte turned to his wife and she gave a nod. 'In the first place,' he told them quietly, 'we do not know if our English cousins will be able to come for us. It is a dangerous enterprise, but as you know, Sir Thomas Welford married your mama's cousin and we have remained close; they have stayed with us here and we have crossed the channel to visit them near Lewes . . . ' he broke off and spoke to his daughter whose expression had changed for an instant. 'You are smiling, Annette, what have I said?'

Annette's face did indeed bear a smile of happy remembrance. 'I remember the last time we went there. I was fourteen and our cousin Luke was eighteen and I fell in love with him. But he took no notice of me, he thought I was just a schoolgirl . . . I am sorry, Papa, it is not the time for romantic memories, please tell us what you wish us to do. Edouard and I are ready, you know.'

'I am glad that you are ready, my dear,' he replied, 'because what I am going to ask you is more than difficult. But first, the general plan. From today, your mama and I will become peasants, we will go and live on the Libette's farm and we will work for them. Henri Libette knows what to do if our English cousins arrive.'

Edouard spoke quickly. 'But what about me? I must care for Annette if you are not there.'

'Edouard,' said his father. 'I want you to be everywhere, but you must be unseen. You must take your horse into the wood at the back of the Maison Charnay and stay in that little hut which the forester uses; Mme Marais will give you food. From there, you will go safely to and from the city to learn what you can, then you can bring any news to the farm. You must be on the lookout for the English visitors and last of all, you will look to Annette.'

'But where will I be, Papa?' Annette sounded worried.

The count stretched out his hand and took hers in his. 'You have a very difficult part to play; are you a good actress?'

The girl beamed a smile. 'I am the best — I can act any part, even a boy.'

'And what about a maid?'

'A maid?' she sounded disappointed. 'But that is not exciting, why should I act the maid?'

'This maid has to act a very important part. Listen carefully. All the maids have been sent home this morning, we have only Mme Marais left in the house. She is our friend and has agreed to help our cause; she will not ally herself to the mob outside. Annette, you must dress as a maid, Mme Marais has the clothes ready for you. You must speak with the Paris

6

slang as the maids do.'

'But that is not difficult, Papa.'

'I have not come to the difficult part. You are to stay in the salon and keep your wits about you. Look out of the window, listen for sounds. You know the sound of the tumbrel, I am sorry to say . . . ' He paused as though he could not go on.

'Annette, when the men bring the tumbrel for us — I think there would be two men, maybe even three — then you are to start acting. They will ask for me and your mama, then you are to sob and cry and tell them that we have already been taken, M. Edouard and Mlle Annette with them. It was yesterday and now the guillotine has them.'

'Le bon Dieu,' said Annette.

'Annette,' reproved her father.

'I am sorry, Papa, it was the shock, but yes, I can do it. If it means that we all be safe then I can do it. But, Papa, it doesn't quite make sense. Are you sure that you have worked it out properly?'

'What do you mean?'

'If I sob and cry, they will think that I am on the side of my employers, the de Charnays, and they will take me, too.'

The count was silent and Annette could see that he was thinking hard. 'You are right, Annette, I did not think of it and I thought I had it all planned efficiently. Now we must reconsider.'

'It is all right, Papa, I think I can do it. I can sob out loud and swear at the de Charnays at the same time. They were good to me and I loved Mlle Annette, but they were like all the landowners and wanted only the privileges of the rich and the king. They did not pay all their taxes, but demanded payment from their serfs at their country estates. Oh, I know that you are not like that, Papa, you are a good landlord and your estate is run properly. You keep all the cottages in good order and your people respect you. They would not wish to see you sent to the guillotine.'

Her father was smiling. 'Goodness gracious, Annette, wherever did you learn all this? I thought you sat all day and did your embroidery and learned your English as your mama wished.'

'I have grown up with the Revolution, Papa. I was only eleven years old when the Bastille was stormed, but I remember it being the start of all the trouble. A lot of things were wrong in our country, I do know that, but there should not be all this butchery of innocent people.' She looked at him. 'Have I convinced you? I will do just as you say while you are with the Libettes and we must hope that cousin Thomas will arrive soon.'

Then she glanced at her brother. 'Where will you be, Edouard? I would wish to have you at my side, but I know that it would be too dangerous. You are the vicomte.'

Edouard put out a hand and touched her arm. 'Annette, I will be only yards away, I promise you, and you must depend on me. I will be there.'

Annette bent and dropped a kiss on his hand. 'I trust you, Edouard.' She turned to her father. 'Are you satisfied, Papa?'

He nodded, but looked sad. 'It seems a lot to ask of a precious daughter. It was the only way we could think of and as Edouard says, he will be there to guard you. Thank you very much, both of you. We must all have courage and perhaps soon, we will be in England and not in this sad country of ours.'

'We have nowhere to live in England, have we?' Edouard asked his father.

'Do not worry, it is all arranged. On our last visit, I could foresee the trouble here and I bought a small house for us in London. Well, it is not quite in London, but very near. The place is called Kensington and I also lodged funds in the bank so we have no need to worry. We can stay there until it is safe to come back to Paris, though it is difficult to see a future for our country at the moment.

There is too much hatred. I think that Robespierre himself will go in the end. But we will not think of these things, we have more immediate worries. Mme Marais — who has been very quiet — has some dresses for you, Annette. Go now and try them on.'

Annette turned to her mother and kissed her. 'Do not worry, Mama. I will do my best and I will become the family heroine!'

Madame la Comtesse's eyes were moist. 'God keep you, my little one,' she whispered and rose and followed her husband from the kitchen.

Edouard turned to Annette; Mme Marais had left to fetch their clothes. 'We will both go and change now,' he told his sister. 'Then I will take what I need into the wood. You stay in the salon and keep watch. Don't forget that Mme Marais will be in the kitchen and that I will be to and fro. As soon as I hear any disturbance, I will wait in the woodshed in the back yard. If I leave the door open a little, I will be able to see what is going on. I know that you will do your best and never forget that I can be with you in seconds.'

Annette nodded. 'Thank you, Edouard. The waiting will be the worst part, but I am sure that I will be able to convince the revolutionaries that all the family have been taken.'

Half an hour later, they parted from each other: Edouard in a roughly woven shirt covered with a leather jerkin and wearing the loose-fitting trousers of the peasant; Annette in a simple dress of brown cotton, her hair tied back with a piece of old ribbon. She appeared strained but composed as she went back into the kitchen to show herself to Mme Marais.

'How do I look, Tante Marais?'

When Annette had been quite young, she had refused to be called 'Mademoiselle Annette' and had reached an agreement with her parents and Mme Marais. She would be called simply Annette and she asked permission to address their good cook as 'tante'. Her father had not objected and over the years, the practice remained.

Mme Marais now looked at the young girl critically. 'Well done,' she said, 'but I think it would be proper for you to have a cap. I have one in the drawer.'

A white cap was arranged over Annette's hair and Mme Marais professed satisfaction. 'It is well, Annette, but can you do this thing which your father asks of you? It is not easy and you will need a great deal of courage as well as pretence.'

Annette looked absurdly proud in her maid's outfit. 'I will do it to save the family. It was a brilliant notion of papa's and I will not let him down. If my English cousin comes, we will soon be safely in England and not here with our heads rolling into the basket like many poor citizens.'

'Annette,' Mme Marais was shocked. 'You cannot say such things.'

'It is the truth. There are many noblemen like papa who gave up their feudal rights and do not demand any of the dues that are owed to them. I have heard him talk of it, but still he is not safe. No one wants to die, Tante Marais, and to die in such a terrible way with the crowds jeering and those awful *tricoteuses* counting the heads . . . '

'Stop it, Annette, you must stop it. You are not old enough to know of these things. How do you come to know what happens at the Place de la Grève, in any case?'

'Edouard told me, he knows everything; some of the students at the university are the worst of all. And when poor King Louis died, Edouard even showed me a print which was circulating. The king standing there with all the soldiers surrounding him and not a space to be found in the crowds. There were even people climbing up on the roofs of the houses to get a good view. One cannot be proud to be French, Mme Marais. I will be glad if we can go to our house in London. They have a good king there and the people are law abiding.'

'I never did, Annette; you speak like a grown girl and here you are not sixteen yet. I suppose it's times like these makes us older and wiser. Now let us be more sensible and no more of this hot air, as they say. What will you do with yourself while we have this dreadful waiting for things to happen?'

'If you have some mending I can do, I will take it into the salon; it would not do for the maid to be found reading Molière or some such author. And I will help you in the kitchen. I must not be idle or I would be imagining all sorts of horrors.'

Annette went into the salon and looked around her. She was accustomed to the gracious furniture, the rich carpet, the priceless paintings. Her father was particularly fond of the works of Fragonard and Annette liked their light-heartedness. It came as quite a shock to her to realize that the room represented all the privileges which the revolutionaries were fighting.

What shall I do, she was asking herself. It doesn't look in the least as though there was a struggle when the men took the family away, though I do suppose that, as the maid, I would have tidied it a little.

She caught sight of the thick curtains of red

and gold brocade and gave a frown; those can go for a start, she muttered to herself. It was an easy task to slide them from their rod and she gave them a shake, folded them and carried them through to the kitchen.

'Whatever next?' asked Mme Marais. 'You've taken the curtains down.'

'It looked too tidy in the salon. Take these to the forester's hut for Edouard; they will help to keep him warm at night. And I think I will hide the clock and one or two of Papa's paintings. I know what I am doing, Tante Marais.'

She left the cook staring in astonishment and returned to the salon. She had always loved the clock which occupied the centre of the mantelpiece over the gracious marble fireplace. Her father had always said that it was of the reign of Louis XIV and had come to him from his grandfather. It was intricately carved from tortoiseshell with an ormolu dial and unusually large numerals of enamel. Annette walked up to it and carefully lifted it down. It was heavy, but she was prepared for that and she looked around to see where she could hide it.

In the corner of the large room was her mother's china cabinet. The two bottom cupboards were neatly carved and the glass-fronted shelves contained the precious

Meissen porcelain figures which the comtesse had collected over the years. Annette had always loved them, her favourite being a small group featuring a young country girl holding a basket and feeding grain to the hens and chicks around her skirt.

Annette looked at it longingly. It is not going to stay here, she told herself, and ran into the kitchen to fetch the strong canvas bag which her father had given her for clothes and the few treasures she was allowed to take to England with her if they succeeded in escaping.

She looked from the porcelain figure to the clock, trying to decide what to do. I would like the little girl and the hens, she said to herself, but it would be easily broken. I will hide it in the cupboard of the cabinet and put the clock in the bottom of the bag. It will be heavy, but that doesn't matter, it will be saved. She hid the piece of porcelain and rearranged the other figures so that there would not be a gap where one was missing.

Then she looked around the room and was satisfied except for the empty grate. I must light a fire if I am going to stay in here, she decided. I have seen Jeanne do it often enough. So she fetched kindling and logs and Mme Marais gave her a lighted taper from the kitchen range; the fire blazed up and she felt pleased with herself.

Edouard came in at that moment and seeing the fire, started to laugh. 'You are making yourself useful, Annette, but whatever happened to the curtains?'

'They were taken by the men who came for the family yesterday,' she replied.

'Are you practising your role, Annette?' he teased her.

'You cannot laugh at such a time and Tante Marais has taken the curtains to your hut; they are to keep you warm at night. Is there any news from the city?'

He shook his head. 'The only news is of rejoicing; there are bonfires everywhere, there would be feasting if there was any food. All because our poor queen has gone to the guillotine.'

Annette looked serious. 'She was never liked, Edouard. From the start she was known as the 'Austrian woman' and she has been so frivolous and extravagant, that it made her very unpopular . . . though I believe King Louis was devoted to her,' she added, as though she should not speak ill of someone who only two days before had undergone the fate they all dreaded. 'Let us speak of more cheerful things. Have you been to see Papa and Mama?'

He smiled. 'You would hardly recognize

them wearing the Libettes' clothes; Papa was chopping firewood and Mama was busy in the dairy. But I believe they worry that they have asked you to do something impossible.'

'Bah,' said Annette. 'I can do it and I have made a start, have I not?'

He looked around him. 'Where is the clock?'

'I have hidden it.'

'Hidden it? Whatever for?' he asked her.

'They can take whatever they like,' she replied stubbornly, 'but they are not having the family clock. Don't forget that it belonged to our great-grandfather.'

He gave her a hug and kissed her. 'You are doing very well and I will come and see you as often as I can. From now on, I will not be any further away that I will not be able to hear a cart coming up the drive.'

'Thank you, Edouard, I am not afraid and I will do my best.'

★   ★   ★

There followed two days of anxious waiting and when the heavy blows finally came on the front door, Annette was in the kitchen and not in the salon. She had supposed that she would hear the approach of the tumbrel.

Mme Marais clasped the young girl to her.

'They have come. Courage, little one.'

Annette said a little prayer and ran to pull back the bolts on the front door. Then she was almost pushed over as three men thrust the door open and entered the house. 'Maurice de Charnay, Comte d'Amand,' said the tallest of them who seemed to be their leader; he was holding a scrap of paper. His clothing was dark but neat, his eyes glared at Annette, his attitude threatening. 'We have come for the comte and his family. Where are they? I have no doubt that they are in hiding, but we will soon find them . . . why are you crying, miss?'

Annette never knew how she achieved it, but she burst into loud sobs and put her hands to her face. 'They are gone to their fate . . . they . . . they were taken yesterday . . . please do not remind me. Why have you come today?'

'It is their turn for Madame la Guillotine; look here, their name is next on the list.' He thrust the piece of paper at her, but she pushed it away with yet more sobs.

'It does not need a piece of paper to tell me that they have gone, I saw it with my own eyes. They were so brave and dignified, it was me who sobbed for them.'

Annette wondered if she had been convincing as she watched them looking at the paper and muttering amongst themselves.

'Frederic, look at this,' said one of them gruffly. 'It says here 'Le Comte d'Amand' and then 'Le Comte d'Amand and family'. But look here, there is a cross against the comte's name, he must have gone yesterday and his family with him. The girl is right.'

Annette felt a grip on her arm from the leader of the group. 'So we come for nothing unless we take the girl; she sobs so much that she must be in sympathy with the family and not with our cause.' He turned to Annette. 'Who are you? Why do you cry so much?'

'I am the maid of the de Charnay family; they have been good to me. Maybe they and their like deserve to die, but when they go, it is like losing one's own family. I weep for them even if it was right for them to go.'

The hold tightened. 'You support M. Robespierre then?' he asked her roughly.

Annette took a deep breath. Now I must save myself, she thought, I must convince them. 'Yes, M. Robespierre, he is right. These aristocratic families, they should not have the privileges; but there you are, people like the de Charnays rob the poor, they do not pay the taxes — '

He interrupted quickly. 'And what does a maid know about it? Tell me that.'

How can I keep this up, Annette was

thinking, but she managed to look at him scornfully. 'Of course I know about them not paying their taxes, everyone knows. It is the tax on our income and they are exempt. We speak of Equality, Monsieur, as well as Liberty and Fraternity; those are the watchwords of the Revolution and the humblest maids in the land know them. You ask Mme Marais, she agrees with everything I say.'

'Mme Marais? Who is she? Is she here?'

'Yes, she is the cook. She is in the kitchen and she still rejoices at the death of the queen the other day.'

The tall man turned to his compatriots. 'You heard what she said, we will let her go; then we will see what the cook can produce for us. Even if we are too late for the family, at least they can give us a good dinner. Frederic, you and Pierre search the house, make sure that there is no one lurking. And bring any pieces or ornaments which take your fancy, we need not go away empty-handed, and they didn't take everything yesterday, they had their hands full.'

He gave a grin and looking around the salon, his eyes became suspicious. 'Where are the curtains?' he asked Annette.

'They were taken yesterday,' she replied calmly.

'And the space on the mantelpiece? A clock, perhaps?'

She nodded. 'Yes, it was the family clock from Louis XIV. I was told always to be careful when dusting it because it was valuable.'

'And that went, too?'

'Yes, and some of the pictures, as many as they could carry.' Annette was gaining confidence.

'There do not seem to be many spaces where there were pictures in here,' he said, looking around him.

She shook her head. 'No, I went and brought some from upstairs to fill the gaps. It didn't look right without the pictures.'

He looked at her. 'You seem to be an honest girl. Now take me to this Mme Marais of yours.'

Annette knew then that she had succeeded; she and Mme Marais were prepared and she knew that the cook would have been standing with the salon door slightly ajar listening to every word which had been said.

But even Annette was not prepared for the reception which Mme Marais gave to the intruders.

In the first place, came the shock that the usually pale and docile cook had rouged her cheeks and was standing tall and belligerent.

'Greetings,' she addressed the man forcefully. 'And why are you here again today? Was not yesterday success enough for you? The whole family of de Charnay at one blow. I trust the crowd roared loudly enough . . . oh, I can see now, you are not the same man as yesterday. What has happened?'

'A mistake, that is all, a simple mistake on the list, but we will not go away empty-handed. My men are fetching what they want from upstairs and there are several pieces of furniture in the big room which will fill the tumbrel. I understand from the girl that you are loyal to us and that we can expect a good meal. How about that then?'

'Only the best for you,' replied Mme Marais. 'You do your gruesome task well. I have a fowl in the pot on the range and can soon add some extra vegetables. All will be ready in twenty minutes. And what about some wine?'

'Madame, I honour you.'

'Go with your men into the salon and I will bring some wine to you, then you can come into the kitchen to eat. You can load up your treasures after your meal.'

The man went off and Annette could hear his heavy footsteps on the stairs. She turned and looked at Mme Marais who held out her arms.

They both cried, but wiped their tears

quickly lest the men returned. 'Annette, my little one, you have succeeded. We will fill them with good food and plenty of wine and they will be on their way.'

'You heard it all, Tante Marais?'

'Yes, I was listening and so was Edouard in case there was trouble; he ran back to the shed when he heard you say that you would bring their leader to me. Edouard will come in again as soon as the men have gone.'

The three who should have been going about their wicked work, sat round the kitchen table and feasted as though they had not eaten for a long time. Another bottle of wine was produced, and when they had loaded up the tumbrel with furniture and pictures, Annette could see that the drink had gone to their legs as well as to their heads. They thanked her for her cooperation and with a roar of '*Vive la République*', whipped up the horse and trundled away from the Maison Charnay.

Annette stood in the window of the salon and the tears rolled down her cheeks.

'My little sister.'

The gentle, proud words from Edouard as he entered the room were too much for her, and she turned and threw herself into his arms, glad to feel them strong about her; her task was done.

# 2

'Annette, Annette,' murmured Edouard as he took off her maid's cap and stroked her hair. 'Come and sit with me on the chaise-longue, at least it was too big for them to take. Cry as much as you like, it has been a strain for you. And as you yourself said, you are a good actress; I heard every word and will never forget what you did. We owe our lives to you. You not only convinced the men, you had the audacity to feed them up with a fine dinner and some wine. When they went away, I was sure that they were quite drunk.'

Annette raised her head. 'Have they really gone? It wasn't hard at the time, but now I seem to be all to pieces. And, Edouard, I am afraid that I could not stop them helping themselves to some of the furniture and the paintings.'

He hugged her. 'What are a Louis XIV cabinet and a few Fragonard paintings compared to our lives? Now, will you be all right if I leave you for a little while? I think that Mme Marais should give you some brandy, I will go and ask her. Then I must hurry over to the farm to tell Papa that all is well. He will think that you are the heroine of the hour and he is right.'

'Thank you for staying with me, Edouard, I am all right now. I will have some dinner with Tante Marais, then perhaps later on, I will ride over and see Mama. Please give her my love.'

Mme Marais had the wisdom to let Annette talk about her experience all through their meal together; at the end of it, Annette felt very tired. She went back into the salon, looked around herself sadly, then brightened when she saw the space on the mantelpiece where the clock had stood. I have saved it, she told herself, we have not lost a lot and we are all safe. She stretched out on the chaise longue and in minutes was fast asleep.

There followed several frustrating days. The count had no idea if their English cousins would come; and if they did arrive, he could not begin to guess when and how they would come. He thought they would have to be in some sort of disguise.

When a farm wagon appeared in the back yard of the house, Mme Marais hurried out to give them directions to the farm. Annette was watching from the kitchen window. The farmer, a thin weakling of a man, dressed in shabby leather and wearing a beret, was not driving the wagon, nor was he doing the talking. His wife at his side was bending over to speak to Mme Marais and Annette thought her an almost fearsome figure. She was enormous for a start; very stout and it could be seen that she was a tall woman even though she was sitting with the reins in her hands.

She was dressed all in black, but her hair could not be seen because of the size of her bonnet which was also black; it was so old that the brim drooped over her face, almost concealing her eyes. Annette wondered that the old woman could see anything, but her vision was obviously good enough to guide the horse.

Then even the wagon itself was odd, thought Annette; it was not large, but it had very deep sides. It was empty save for a heap of some unknown farm stuff covered with a thick and tattered cloth; this was the only bright thing about the strangers for it was a red and green checked cloth almost like a blanket.

Annette was wondering why they had come to the house when it was obviously the farm they wanted; she was not left guessing for long for she saw the old woman straighten up, say a few words to her husband and drive out of the yard.

Mme Marais came hurrying back into the

kitchen. 'A strange couple, the farmer didn't say a word except 'bon jour', but his wife made up for it. Your father had ordered a feeding trough for the Libettes' farm, it was in the wagon, did you see it? They should have been here days ago, but were held up at the North Gate because they had told the guard that they were looking for the Maison Charnay. They were afraid for their lives when the guard told them that the family had gone to the guillotine; it was only when they insisted — I suppose I should say that *she* insisted for I've never seen a poorer creature than her husband — that they had something to deliver to the farm that they were allowed through. She did thank me very politely when I put her in the direction of the farm.'

'Perhaps our next visitor will be our cousin,' said Annette forlornly.

'Have patience, my dear. We are all safe, that is the most important thing.'

Annette looked at her. 'What are you going to do when we go to England, Tante Marais?'

Mme Marais smiled. 'Do not worry, it is all arranged. Mme Libette wishes to enlarge the poultry farm and the dairy; she is very hard-working, but is idle in the house and does not like to cook. She has always been a good friend to me and she has asked me to go as her housekeeper and cook. Her children are now grown up and married so there is plenty of room in the farmhouse. It will not be very much money, but that does not worry me. I will be busy and I will have a nice home so I could not ask for more. I could wish for peace in our poor country, but it is hard to imagine a peaceful land with the Committee of Public Safety in power. But we will not think of such things. We have to be patient and see what is going to happen; and we must hope that the revolutionaries do not return here.'

'I think they would have come straight away if there had been any trouble,' said Annette. 'It may be that the men took their treasures to their homes and then went on to fetch whichever poor soul was next on their list. It is too dreadful to think about, I long to be safely in England.'

She sat thinking longingly of her English relations. Sir Thomas Welford was a widower and his wife had been cousin to Annette's mother; so it was that his children were only second cousins to herself and Edouard.

She had admired Marianne, who was the eldest of the cousins, but it was Luke she remembered best. She wondered if he would be there for in the last letter they had received, there was mention of Luke going to Oxford.

The next girl was Lucy and the two had become good friends; in her heart, Annette had done some matchmaking between Edouard and Lucy, but she knew that Edouard would have to find his way in England before allowing himself to think of romance and marriage.

It was almost as though Annette's thoughts had conjured up her brother for a few minutes later, an excited Edouard burst into the salon, grabbed her hands to pull her up and whisk her around.

'Annette, they have come. Our cousin has sent someone to take us to England. The oddest pair you ever saw . . . a great big farm woman dressed all in black with a little man for a husband who just nods his head and doesn't say a word . . . what is it, Annette?' Edouard could see that his sister was staring at him in disbelief.

'Edouard, stop, stop, you are mistaken. They were here asking for directions to the farm. I saw them from the window while Mme Marais talked to them. I would recognize them anywhere from your description, but they said that they were delivering something to the farm. I saw it in the back of the wagon, covered with a blanket or rug. They can't be from England, I could hear the old woman speaking; it was a kind of patois with no hint of an English accent.'

Edouard was laughing at her. 'You don't trust them, you think they are going to take us straight to the guillotine. But you are wrong, Annette, for they have brought a letter from Sir Thomas Welford, our cousin. Papa has no doubts for they have always corresponded and he knows Sir Thomas's handwriting.'

'What does the letter say?' Annette still sounded doubtful.

'It introduces Monsieur and Madame Bézier; Cousin Thomas says that it is not safe for him to come himself as he does not speak the French language well enough. M. and Mme Bézier are from the south of France and can be trusted; it is not the first time they have taken a family to England and they know exactly what they have to do. It was a relief to them to find Papa and Mama still alive for they had been told that the family had already gone to the guillotine. Our cousin leaves it to them to make their own way and to use any necessary disguises for us; we cannot travel as the de Charnays, it would not be safe.'

Annette smiled at last. 'It is true, I believe you for I could hear her southern patois. But suddenly I feel afraid. And I must leave Tante Marais, too. What do you wish us to do? Is it safe to leave her here on her own?'

Edouard shook his head. 'No, it is not. Has she told you that she is going to live with the Libettes as their housekeeper?'

'Yes, I am pleased for her, she has no family of her own in Paris.'

'Papa says that you are to pack what you need in the canvas bag he gave you, he will buy you new clothes when we reach London; and Mme Marais is to bring her portmanteau, I think she has had it packed in readiness for a long time now. Shall we go and tell her?'

'But how are we to get to the farm, Edouard?'

'I will drive you in the trap, my horse can be tied to the back, that is no trouble. Come along quickly, we must not lose time as Mme Bézier wants to reach the coast before dark.'

It was all confusion and rush after that. They arrived at the farm to find the comte talking earnestly to Mme Bézier; they were standing by the wagon. The old woman was pointing, the count was frowning. Then he started to laugh and Edouard and Annette looked at him in astonishment.

'What is it, Papa?' asked Annette.

He looked at them. 'You are both safely here, that is good. Mme Bézier has been explaining to me her disguise for us, but I am afraid that you will not be pleased Edouard, for yours is the difficult part this time.'

'I will do anything to save us,' Edouard replied readily. 'Somehow we have to get past the guard; the Béziers did not find it easy and there were only the two of them.'

The count turned to Mme Bézier, who now that she could be seen standing was indeed a large woman, but slightly bent and not as tall as Annette had imagined.

'It is a dangerous game we play,' she told them in her broad patois. 'We will not go through the North Gate for that is the worst. Our sailing boat waits for us near Dieppe so we must take the Dieppe road; it is safer than the Calais road which most émigrés take to escape to London. Dieppe is also nearer to Newhaven where Sir Thomas Welford will meet you with his carriage.'

She sounded most composed and Annette began to have confidence; the old woman's face was still half hidden, but she did not hesitate as she spoke, with a high cracked voice which sounded odd coming from one so large. 'Now your father will tell you what you have to do,' she continued. 'Then the good Libettes will give us a meal and we will be off. Monsieur,' she said and looked at the count.

He was looking particularly at Edouard

and took both brother and sister closer to the wagon which was standing outside the farmhouse door. It looked just as Annette had seen it earlier, still with its peculiar cloth in place.

'Gaston, come here.' Mme Bézier turned to her husband who was standing with the horse.

Annette watched in amazement as the little man jumped up on to the wagon; he might be a man of few words, but he is nimble enough, she thought.

He took hold of the cloth and threw it over the side of the wagon; sure enough, underneath it, and in a large wooden box was the farm trough. He lifted out the trough and handed it to his wife who let it drop to the ground; she did not take her eyes off him.

They all watched without a word as he turned the long empty crate over; they could see that it was of polished wood and had a smooth lid.

Annette's words broke from her. 'It looks like a coffin.'

A cackle came from the old woman. 'You are quite right, it *is a coffin*. Show them, Gaston.'

He lifted the lid carefully and they all peered inside as though they were expecting a magic trick; but all they could see was that the so-called coffin was quite empty and it did not have a base to it. It was lying on the floor of the wagon and for some unknown reason, a big square hole had been cut in the wagon floor so that the ground was showing underneath.

Annette gave a shudder. 'What does it mean, Papa?'

The count put an arm around her, but addressed himself to his son. 'Edouard, I regret to tell you that you are going to have to play the corpse. Mme Bézier insists that she can get us safely out of France if we are a funeral party. Edouard, you will lie flat in the coffin with your face to the hole in the floor of the wagon to enable you to breathe. You will be able to see the road underneath, but that does not matter.'

He paused. 'Now listen carefully; if we are stopped by guards, you will hear them shouting. You are to turn over immediately, draw the cloth which I am going to put inside the coffin over you and lie perfectly still. It will be only for a few minutes, I trust, because we are going to say that you are our beloved son and that you have died of a fever, though the doctor did not think it was the smallpox. We come from Dieppe and we are going home to bury you. I imagine that they will shut the lid quickly at the mention of smallpox; you can turn over again and we can be on our way. Do you understand all that? Can you do it?'

Edouard was grinning. 'I do not think it will be difficult. But what about you and Mama and Annette?'

The count put his arm around his wife and Annette. 'The two of you are heartbroken. You are to sit on your canvas bags at the side of the coffin and make your eyes red with weeping. That is not difficult, eh?'

They both nodded solemnly and Annette said quietly, 'We will do our best, Papa, and what about you?'

'I am going to sit between M. and Mme Bézier. The guards may choose to think that I am her husband, but I will leave any talking to her. She can talk enough for the two of us, I think, and my voice would give me away. Do you all understand? If you are happy with the arrangement, we will have our meal and be on our way.'

Not one of them could have said that they were happy, but all felt that the plan was foolproof and went into the farmhouse where they enjoyed a good dinner of mutton cooked with carrots and onions, with plenty of home-baked bread to have with it.

Annette bade a tearful farewell to Mme Marais and they all thanked the Libettes. The coloured blanket was folded at the bottom of the coffin for Edouard to lie on and a piece of unbleached linen was laid on top of him. Annette and her mother were given warm woollen shawls to wrap around them and they climbed into the wagon. The count handed them their canvas bags to sit on and grimaced as he picked up Annette's.

'Whatever are you taking to England, Annette,' he asked her.

'It feels very heavy.'

'It is the clock,' she stated.

'The clock?' Her father was mystified.

'Yes, Papa, I have wrapped great-grandpapa's clock in my dress. We couldn't leave it behind, it is very precious to us.'

He gave her a kiss. 'I did not think that I would smile today, but it was a lovely thought of yours, Annette, and I thank you very much.'

He climbed up to sit between Mme Bézier and her husband and they were off.

The first part was easy enough; through the farm and the parkland of the de Charnay estate, then they took the lane towards Paris. Mme Bézier was careful to avoid the road which would take them through the heart of the city and the notorious North Gate.

Annette let herself lean across the coffin, but the road was pot-holed and she wondered

36

how poor Edouard was surviving the bumpy ride.

They succeeded in finding the road to St Germain and the highway which went directly to Dieppe. And here it was that they found themselves in a line of carts, carriages and wagons, all of them being inspected by the busy guards who looked efficient in their uniforms and tricorne hats.

As each vehicle approached, the guard would mutter 'pass' and those fortunate people would be on their way.

Annette could see from where she sat that the carriage in front of them was a rather grand affair and with four horses; she could not imagine that a nobleman's carriage would be allowed out of the city.

Then she saw the coachman bend down and give the guard a slip of paper. The guard looked at the paper and peered into the carriage and she heard the words 'lawyer, pass'. Annette watched as the carriage was driven away; she knew that most lawyers supported the Revolution.

But now it was their turn; she suddenly felt cold and started to shiver. Her mother noticed and putting out a caring hand, wrapped the thick shawl more closely round her daughter.

'Have courage, little one,' she whispered.

The guard came up to them and looked at them suspiciously. 'You have a pass?' he asked Mme Bézier who held her whip stiffly and sat very upright.

'We do not need a pass for a funeral,' was her reply.

'A funeral is it? And why do you need to go out of Paris to bury your dead?'

'Our family grave is in Dieppe, we are taking our loved one there.'

'So who is it that you carry?'

'Our son . . . our dear son.'

Annette heard the old woman's voice falter; surely she is not going to cry, the young girl thought.

'So,' stated the guard. 'This is your husband sitting next to you, and the others, who are they?'

'You ask a lot of questions, young man,' said Mme Bézier.

'It is my duty; too many of our noble families are escaping into England. We take every precaution.'

'If it will quicken our journey out of Paris, I will introduce our family. Our poor Louis lies in the coffin, and his young wife grieves for him. She is weeping now, as you see.'

'And the other two?'

'Her father sits next to my husband and her mother comforts her the best she can. Are you satisfied, monsieur?'

The guard walked round the wagon.

Annette trembled, and then, as her mother put an arm around her, she felt the shock of a sharp pinch on her arm.

'Ow . . . ' she cried out and hastily changed it to a wail, then without any effort on her part, she broke into a paroxysm of weeping.

'So,' the guard said stiffly. 'We have the young widow. We have the coffin. But I am wondering if it is a coffin or whether it is just an empty box. We are used to that trick, I might tell you.'

Mme Bézier turned round to him. 'You desecrate the dead, but you are at liberty to lift the lid and see that our poor son lies stiff and still for ever. He had the fever and the doctor did not know if it was the smallpox. Within a week, poor Louis was dead.'

The guard stiffened at the word smallpox, but he summoned a younger man. 'Climb into the wagon and lift the lid of the coffin, you can loosen it with your knife if it is nailed down.'

'No, you cannot,' cried out Annette. 'My husband . . . you cannot disturb his final resting place.'

Then she regretted her outburst for it seemed to make the guard more suspicious.

'We will see what we find, madame,' he said to her.

The lid of the coffin was raised by only a few inches; there came a dreadful stench and the younger guard dropped the lid with a bang.

'Please, sir, the body is stinking, it is covered with a cloth, but I can see his boots. Do you want to see?'

The guard took a few steps back. 'There is nothing wrong with my sense of smell, thank you.' He turned to Mme Bézier. 'In God's name, how long is it since he died?'

He did not know of the complete bewilderment of the de Charnay family. The count turned round, Annette looked at her mother and they were all asking themselves the same question. Whatever could Edouard have done to produce such a deadly effect? Was he all right, they wondered?

But Mme Bézier was upset by nothing. 'He has been dead three days. We had to wait to have the coffin made, there is a terrible demand for coffins. Now do you understand our haste to get to Dieppe before nightfall? Can we proceed?'

The guard stood still. 'You had better go quickly, my commiserations to you and your family, ma'am.'

Mme Bézier cracked the whip and they

were off. The wagon moved slowly along the crowded road, but all of them were over-joyed at their success.

'Thank God,' said the countess. 'We are free.'

Annette crept closer to her, she was still shivering and felt ill with the anxiety of all that had taken place; she was glad of her mother's arms around her. 'Can Edouard come out now?' she asked.

Mme Bézier heard the question. 'Stay where you are, all of you, we are not out of Paris yet. I will stop when we get to the forest of St Germain. It is only ten minutes.'

She was right about the forest and drove the wagon on to a broad track which ran through the trees. As they stopped, she turned and jumped from her driving perch into the wagon; she opened the lid of the coffin. '*Sacré bleu*, M. Edouard,' she swore at him coarsely. 'What have you done?'

Edouard sat up smiling, his face almost black with mud and grime. 'Is it safe? Where are we? Can I get up?' He threw the cloth to one side, stretched his legs and climbed out of the coffin. He laughed. 'You had better not come too near. Did I not stink to high heaven? Did it succeed in putting the guards off their search?'

The count stood with him. 'It was a stroke

41

of genius, Edouard, but how did you manage it?'

'It was easy and I thought of it on the spur of the moment. As we left the farmyard, I was face-down looking through the hole in the bottom of the wagon and we went over some trodden down horse dung. I put out a hand and managed to get some and I threw it to the bottom of the coffin near my feet. The smell was dreadful, but at least I had some air through the hole.' He paused and looked at them.

'Then I lay quiet, but I heard everything when you were stopped by the guards and I turned over and lay quite still as you had told me to do. I just had to hope that the guard would not see the dung, I pulled the cloth up so that he would just be able to see my feet. It worked, did it not? I heard what he said before he shut the lid again. And then the relief as we drove on, it was all worth the smell and a dirty face! I feel as though I am caked with mud.'

Annette hugged him in spite of the smell. 'You are the hero now, Edouard. It was very quick thinking on your part.' She turned to Mme Bézier who seemed to be beaming under the black bonnet. 'What do we do now, madame?'

'Edouard must go back in the box until we

42

are through St Germain, then I will strike twice with my whip and he can get out until we approach Dieppe.' She climbed back on to her seat. 'After Dieppe, it is only a mile or two before we reach the boat.'

Edouard did as he was told and they all resumed their positions. Annette felt colder than ever and the countess noticed that she was shivering and put a hand to the girl's forehead.

'Annette, you are shivering, but your skin is burning. Do you have a fever?'

'I don't know, Mama, perhaps it is just the upset of our journey. I will lay my head on Edouard's coffin.'

St Germain was not a large town and they drove through it without difficulty; it seemed a peaceful place after Paris and there were no guards to be seen.

Once out of the town, Mme Bézier did as she had said and struck the coffin twice with her whip. Edouard climbed out and sat with Annette, his arms around her to try and keep her warm.

The good Mme Bézier stopped at the next bridge and gave Edouard time to run down to the river and dash water over his dirty face. Minutes later, he was back in the wagon and bending over Annette who seemed to be almost unaware of what was going on.

'Mama,' said Edouard. I am afraid that Annette has the fever. It is something more than worry over the events of the last few days.'

'We will hold her,' replied the countess. 'She will be more comfortable; are you all right, Annette?'

'The clock has gone,' said Annette and her mother noticed that the girl's eyes did not seem to be focused.

'She is talking nonsense,' the countess said to Edouard and he nodded and looked worried.

By the time they had reached Neufchâtel, a small town not very far short of Dieppe, it became obvious that Annette was not at all well. She shivered continually in spite of being wrapped in two thick shawls; when she spoke, none of her words made sense though she did say 'Edouard' continually.

Outside the town, Mme Bézier stopped the wagon and turned to the count. 'Monsieur, I do not think it wise that Mlle Annette should travel further. We need to seek out a doctor for her. It is a dilemma for the boat awaits us beyond Dieppe. What do you wish me to do?'

The count climbed down from his seat and went to speak to his wife and Edouard. He stroked Annette's forehead and frowned. She opened her eyes at his touch and seemed to

44

know him. 'Papa,' she said. 'Edouard is dead.'

'No, no, sweetheart, Edouard is here, he is holding your hand.' He turned to his wife. 'What shall we do? She is not fit to travel any further today.'

The countess had tears in her eyes. 'Poor Annette, it is all the worry and she has been so brave. We must rely on Mme Bézier.'

Their driver came and stood at the side of the wagon. She had heard what had been said by the family, but it was a long time before she made any comment. Then she spoke slowly.

'We cannot keep the boat waiting, that much is certain. What I suggest is this, Monsieur, as you are good enough to ask me. In Neufchâtel, I know of an inn which is used by those escaping the Terror. It is usually quite safe and I believe that it would be better to stop here and not to go on to Dieppe; they are more for the Revolution there. But the boat is the problem. I can only suggest that Edouard takes his mother on to England — I will conduct them there — and that you stay at Le Coq d'Or with Mlle Annette. The landlord, M. Richet will fetch a doctor and Mme Richet will care for Mlle Annette.'

The count looked concerned. 'That is helpful, Mme Bézier, but how will we get Annette to England when she is better?'

Mme Bézier spoke firmly. 'Your wife must tell Sir Thomas Welford what has happened and he will arrange everything as soon as you send a message saying that Annette is well enough to travel. M. Edouard will return to France for his sister and no doubt, M. Bézier and myself will be there to take you all safely to England. I do not think it wise that the countess should come back for Annette, so perhaps it can be arranged so that M. Edouard has a young lady to accompany him to Neufchâtel. Mlle Annette will need female company.'

The count stared at Mme Bézier; here was a sensible head on humble shoulders, he told himself. No wonder she had been successful in so many escapes to England. He knew that he must agree with her suggestions and went around to the back of the wagon to tell his wife and Edouard of the plan.

The countess cried at the thought of leaving Annette, but she was a practical woman and could see the sense of it all.

And so they drove up to Le Coq d'Or in Neufchâtel. The count went in to see if there were rooms for himself and Annette and to find out if there was anyone who could care for her.

He came back very satisfied.

By this time, Annette hardly seemed aware

of her surroundings and she was carried into the inn and put into a bed in a small room; her mother kissed her and said goodbye in a flood of tears, though she was reassured by the sensible maid who had been found to sit with Annette.

'Madame, please do not worry. My name is Marie Hébert and I have nursed my own children through many a fever. I will take great care of your daughter for you.'

Edouard at last persuaded his mother that Mme Bézier was anxious to proceed to Dieppe. They left Annette with their father on one side of the bed and the maid on the other; she continually bathed the girl's burning face with pads of cool, wet flannel. Annette did not know that her mother and Edouard had gone.

# 3

Dieppe was negotiated without difficulty. The coffin had been dispensed with at the inn at Neufchâtel and replaced with a crate of noisy hens. In the back of the wagon, Edouard held on to the crate and his mother sat on the driving seat supported by M. and Mme Bézier. The countess was in a sad way.

Edouard had a bottle of cognac in his hand and sang and shouted noisily. There was a solitary guard at the west gate of the town; he held a firearm, but was not in uniform. He gratefully accepted a swig from Edouard's bottle and had a short conversation with Mme Bézier. He believed without question that they were going to stay with their relations at St Pierre-sur-Mer and waved them on their way.

They travelled along a very poor road within sight of the sea until they reached the tiny fishing village of St Pierre-sur-Mer. Before they entered the village, Mme Bézier spoke to Edouard.

'M. Edouard, you must look to your mother. There will be a rowing boat waiting for us and we will be taken as quickly as possible to our yacht, the *Marie Rose*. I hope it will be waiting in the bay. St Pierre is a very small and quiet place and I think we will be safe, but we take no risks.'

'But what about you and M. Bézier?' asked Edouard.

'Do not worry. The wagon will be hidden behind the cottages in the village until we need it again; we have good friends in St Pierre. We will come to England with you to await our orders.'

Edouard looked curious. 'Do you speak English, Mme Bézier?'

He sensed her grin rather than saw it. 'I speak a few words, but M. Bézier, he was a servant to English gentlemen on their grand tour and he speaks it well. In France, he pretends to be a quiet man; in England, he is the spokesman. I think I can trust you with this, M. Edouard?'

'Yes, of course, I will do everything you tell me.'

'We will stay at an inn at Newhaven — it is difficult to say, that one! — while we send a message to your cousin and he will bring his carriage for you and your mama.'

'And what will you do then?'

'We will stay in Newhaven to await our orders, that is all I can say.'

Edouard looked worried. 'Mme Bézier, we

must repay you for your kindness. We owe our lives to you and your husband.'

Again the grin. 'Do not worry, M. Edouard, your good father has done all that is necessary.'

'I hope you have not put yourselves under suspicion,' he said to her.

She gave a chuckle. 'You do not know how clever our disguises are, next time you would not recognize us. We are well rewarded and when the Terror is over, Gaston and I can retire to our little house near Montpellier where we can live in comfort and hope to forget these terrible times. Now we will look for the rowing boat.'

Edouard had no difficulty in guiding his mother over the sandy beach to the waiting boat; they could see the sails of the yacht anchored not far off the shore. It was now dark and Edouard wondered if they would sail through the night.

The countess was thinking the same. 'It is getting dark, Edouard, do you think we shall reach England tonight? I cannot wait to be with my dear cousin there. It has broken my heart to leave Annette so ill.'

'She has my father with her, Mama, try not to worry.'

The sea was a little choppy, but Edouard could only think what a good thing it was that the wind blew strong enough to carry them over to England.

Willing hands helped them up the ladder on to the yacht and the countess managed very well. They were given drinks and made comfortable below, leaving M. and Mme Bézier leaning over the rail and looking at the darkening water.

When they reached Newhaven, it was first light and the fishing boats were putting out; they waited for another rowing boat and in minutes, they were ashore and being welcomed by the landlord of the Boar's Head, only yards from the small harbour.

'What do we do now?' the countess asked faintly as they sat themselves down to a breakfast in a small, private sitting-room.

'I have said goodbye to M. and Mme Bézier, Mama, and I have thanked them. But for them, I do not think we would be here today.' Edouard tried to sound cheerful.

'But Maurice and Annette are not here,' said his mother plaintively.

'Try not to worry. Annette is in good hands and they will be brought to safety just as we have been. Now we must wait for our cousin; apparently a boy has gone with a message and as you know, our cousin's house is not far from Newhaven. I am certain that he will come with all haste.'

He was pleased to see that his mother had sat back in her chair and gone to sleep after they had finished their breakfast; he, himself, stood at the window and watched the activity outside as the small port awakened.

By mid-morning, he saw a carriage pull up and guessed that it was his cousin.

He woke his mother and she seemed a little bewildered. But there came a tap on the door, and a tall, rather heavy gentleman entered the room. He did not wear a wig and his greying hair was tied back; he looked to be nearing fifty years of age and was of distinguished appearance.

'Caroline,' he said with a broad smile as he held out his hands to the countess.

Her face lit up and she rose from the chair to run forward into his arms. 'Thomas, my dear cousin,' she said in English.

★   ★   ★

A week previously, Sir Thomas Welford had been told that their cousins from Paris were hoping to be in England very soon.

Sir Thomas had been a widower for two years and relied on his housekeeper, Mrs Franklyn, to see to the smooth running of Welford Grange. His ancestral home was a large Elizabethan manor in Sussex and not far from Lewes; it was half-timbered for the most part and would be described as rambling rather than imposing. His estate was extensive and included three farms as well as many acres of beautiful parkland which stretched as far as the nearest village of Sapstead.

Sir Thomas had helped to organize the flight of his cousins from Paris; they were of no blood relation to himself, for the Comtesse de Charnay had been Caroline Vilven and a first cousin of his wife. Nevertheless, he was fond of his French relations and eager to see them escape the horrors of the Revolution in France.

His only son, Luke, was up at Oxford, but Sir Thomas had taken his two eldest daughters, Marianne and Lucy, into his confidence regarding the French family.

Marianne, at twenty-one, was the eldest of his children and while not regarded as a beauty, her fair skin, deep auburn hair and dark eyes made her striking. Her younger sister, Lucy, at eighteen, was the beauty of the family; she had inherited her father's dark hair and her mother's blue eyes. The two sisters were very close.

As soon as their father had told them of the expected arrival of their cousins from France, the two girls had been impatiently on the lookout for a carriage on the drive; they had somehow imagined that the émigrés would arrive secretly and in disguise. Sir Thomas had forgotten to mention that he would be driving to Newhaven to meet the family as soon as he had word.

The only regular visitor to Welford Grange, and he came on the same day as Marianne and Lucy had been told the news of the de Charnay family, was Mr Harvey Burrage-Smith.

Mr Burrage-Smith was a Member of Parliament; he lived at Broadoaks, a modest dwelling built at the time of George I, which was situated between the Welford estate and Sapstead village. He was the Welfords' nearest neighbour and Marianne had known him all her life; he was undeniably good-looking, but she never thought of him as exceptionally handsome. His dark hair was carelessly styled, his eyes grey and his mouth generous but firm, not given to much laughter.

Marianne was betrothed to him, but she was not certain if she loved him; sometimes she thought him dull, she suspected his politics and regarded him to be too seriously devoted to his life as a Member of Parliament.

But her parents had wished for the match, she had met no one who pleased her better and she decided that she could be comfortably married to him. At the back of her mind, she had a young lady's wish for romance and excitement, but before the death of her mother, she had concluded that romance was not to be for her and had pleased Lady Welford by agreeing to becoming betrothed to Harvey.

There were two much younger members of the Welford family, Alice and Rose, who were still in the schoolroom under the direction of the Welford governess, Miss Biddisham, who had never been called other than 'Biddy'.

On the morning of Harvey's visit to see Marianne, Biddy had complained of the headache and Lucy had gone up to the schoolroom to help the children with their reading.

Marianne was in the drawing-room, excited at the imminent arrival of her cousins from France; she was wondering if she would have her usual ride out with no Lucy to accompany her.

When Harvey was announced, she was surprised. She had seen him only the day before when they had gone riding together in the direction of Cliffe Hill and had enjoyed a gallop. Marianne found that she seemed to be more at ease with Harvey when they were out riding together; he appeared to lose some of his stiffness and when he helped her to dismount, he always had a smile in his eyes.

In the drawing-room, he was different and that morning was no exception. He entered and bowed formally; he was not in riding clothes and she assumed that he had come over from Broadoaks in his carriage. He always dressed well; that morning, he was wearing a fitted coat of brown face cloth, shaped to the waist and with long tails. He wore knee breeches and pale silk stockings, his cravat was tied in a full bow; she thought that this made him look less severe. Like her father, he wore his hair unpowdered and it was shaped thick and dark to his head.

Why cannot I like him more, Marianne was thinking as he made his bow and took her hand. Most girls would think themselves fortunate to have such a fine gentleman as their prospective husband.

'Marianne, my dear,' he was saying once they were seated. Their chairs were placed near the fire for it was a cold October morning and the blazing logs gave out a cheerful warmth. 'I have come to bid you farewell for a little while.'

'You are needed in the House?' she asked; his political life intrigued her for she sometimes thought it very dull for such an intelligent man as Harvey Burrage-Smith.

He ignored her question. 'I will probably be in London some of the time; I find the sessions in the House tedious.'

'Perhaps you will be entertaining feminine company in London,' she said and was immediately appalled. How could she have said such a thing?

When his rebuke came, she was not surprised.

'Marianne, that is not the kind of remark I expect from you, they were certainly not the words of a lady. I trust you will not speak so rashly once we are married.'

'No, no, of course not, Harvey, I am sorry. I don't know what made me say it. I am really quite excited today.'

He raised his eyebrows, but his expression did not change. 'You are? And why, might I ask, is that?'

'I am not sure that I should tell you, though of course, you will learn soon enough.'

'You speak as though it is something of which I will not approve.'

I will never get to know him, Marianne thought, but launched into her explanation. 'I always have the feeling that you are in favour of the Revolution in France; you associate with the younger Whigs and we all know what Mr Fox's attitude to the Revolution is — '

'That is enough, Marianne, I do not expect my future wife to air political views.'

'But I am marrying a politician,' she replied, her voice raised.

'My place is in Parliament, yours is in the home. I hope you will remember that.'

Before Marianne could begin to object to his words, he continued with a question. 'And what is it that has caused you so much excitement and outspokenness today?'

'My father has told us that our cousins are being brought over from France. It is very secret, but of course, you will know about it when they arrive. You know of our family connection with the Comte d'Amand, for you have met my cousins before. They came over for poor Mama's funeral. You remember Edouard and Annette? Edouard is very handsome.'

'I trust that you do not fall in love with the handsome French cousin, Marianne.'

There was an odd tone in his voice and Marianne looked at him searchingly. 'What are you saying, Harvey, I am going to marry you.'

His hand shot out and she felt a hard grasp on her arm through the long sleeves of the muslin gown she was wearing. 'And do you love me?' he asked brusquely. 'Are you telling me that you love me? We have never spoken of love between us.'

Marianne knew that this was true for their intended marriage had been a long-standing arrangement between her parents and Harvey. 'I am very fond of you, Harvey,' she said tentatively. She could not pretend a love she did not feel.

'I am glad to hear it, my dear.' His reply was caustic and continued, 'For I am fond of you, too . . . Marianne . . . '

She looked up quickly, his voice had suddenly changed.

'What is it?' she asked him.

'Oh nothing, nothing at all. Perhaps one day I will be able to make you love me.'

'That is an odd thing to say.' Marianne could feel a strangeness in his mood.

'Maybe it is, but I repeat what I said. Don't fall in love with your cousin, Marianne, you are mine.'

She ignored the last words and smiled at him. 'You need not fear, Harvey, I have it all planned. Edouard will do nicely for Lucy. Don't you think that is a good idea?'

'Maybe,' he smiled and looked a little less fierce. 'You are right in thinking that I support the Revolution, but I cannot extend my political views to the relatives of the girl I am going to marry. Now I must say goodbye for a se'nnight or two. Might I ask you for a kiss?'

Why does he have to ask, thought Marianne? Could he not just take me in his arms and kiss me without asking my permission? But she hid her feelings and as he helped her to her feet, she lifted her face to his.

His lips on hers were firm and brief, she liked his touch but she felt no stir of her feelings. Harvey Burrage-Smith walked from the room leaving a somewhat disappointed bride-to-be.

Then passed an anxious week of watching and waiting. The two sisters rode out each morning and sat at their embroidery or the pianoforte in the afternoon. They talked a lot of their French cousins whom they could remember well. Annette de Charnay had been no more than a schoolgirl on their last visit, but Lucy, sixteen at the time, remembered Edouard as a handsome young gentleman who paid her little attention.

As the de Charnay family had come over for the funeral of Lady Welford, there had been little merrymaking, but the cousins had enjoyed each other's company. Lucy particularly remembered practising her French with Annette; the de Charnay children had grown up with an English mother and although they usually conversed in French, their command of the English language was perfect.

Marianne and Lucy talked about them endlessly.

'It is a pity that you are betrothed to Harvey, Marianne,' said Lucy one day when they were quietly riding through the park.

'Why do you say that?' asked Marianne, looking at her younger sister who looked fetching in a blue riding-dress and a jaunty, feathered hat.

'I have the feeling that you and Edouard would suit,' replied Lucy with an air of mischief.

Marianne laughed. 'He is too young for me and I cannot let Harvey down.'

'But you don't love Harvey.' Lucy made the observation as though it was her carefully considered opinion.

'How do you know that I don't love Harvey?' asked Marianne.

'I can tell by the way you behave when you are with him. He doesn't love you either, unless he is hiding it very carefully. You are just good friends. I would want more than that from the gentleman whom I was to marry.'

'What do you know about it all, young lady?' Marianne was looking at her sister with a teasing smile.

Lucy had no hesitation in speaking her mind. 'I would know straight away if I loved someone. I would feel the thrill of love and would want him to kiss me.'

Marianne laughed even more heartily this time. 'You have been reading the romances of Mrs Radcliffe. Papa lets you buy them in Lewes.'

Lucy nodded. 'Yes, I have just finished *A Sicilian Romance*.'

Marianne became more serious. 'I don't think life is like that, Lucy, but I will let you dream your dreams. And I have plans for you.'

'What do you mean?'

'It is simple. You and Edouard! What could be more romantic? One day you would become the Comtesse d'Amand and the Revolution would be over, and you could go back to France and live in a château.'

It was Lucy's turn to laugh, but she pretended to be cross. 'Now you are roasting me and you say that I am too romantic! In any case, the de Charnay country estate does not have a château. I can remember Annette telling me that it has a big house near Belfort. It is nearly in Switzerland.' She paused silently for a moment. 'I wonder if they will soon be here? It is very trying on the patience and we have the worry of not knowing if they can be brought to England in safety.'

Their impatience and worry was brought to an end two days later when Sir Thomas received a message from Newhaven and set off in the carriage.

Marianne and Lucy were standing at the drawing-room window when the Welford carriage was brought up to the front door; then their excitement turned to mystification as only a young gentleman and an older lady alighted. Sir Thomas walked with them to the door and brought them into the drawing-room. Marianne saw immediately that they were both dressed humbly as a farmer's wife and her son would have been.

'Aunt Caroline . . . ' stammered Marianne. She could see that her aunt was red-eyed and upset. 'What is it? Where are my uncle and Annette?' Although the count and countess were her cousins, she had always called them aunt and uncle.

The countess put her arm around the girl. 'It is so good to be here. Your father will tell you.'

Marianne took her to a chair near the fire then turned round to greet Edouard. She gave a start of astonishment.

In the middle of the room, Lucy and Edouard were holding hands and gazing at each other, then Edouard sat Lucy in the chair next to his mother; his hand was still on Lucy's shoulder as though to calm her.

They have fallen in love on sight, thought Marianne; I might have guessed it would happen, but I must pay attention to what Papa has to say.

A maid had brought in coffee and brandy and Sir Thomas was persuading his cousin to take some small sips of brandy before drinking her coffee.

He turned to Marianne and Lucy. 'I am afraid that it is not good news. The family reached Neufchâtel safely, it is not far from Dieppe, but Annette became ill. Caroline tells me that she has had to leave her there with Maurice. The yacht was waiting to bring them to England so Edouard has come on ahead with his mother. A message will be sent to us when Annette is well enough to travel and Edouard will go back for her. The illness is not a serious one, but the greater danger is that the count is still in France.' He put his arm round the countess. 'Caroline, be sure that you will be well comforted here with my two girls. They will take good care of you.'

Caroline de Charnay managed a tearful smile. 'Thank you, all of you. I could not be in a better place at this dreadful time. I know our prayers will be answered and Maurice will soon bring Annette safely here.'

The countess retired early that night and with the young people being left on their own, Edouard was able to tell Marianne and Lucy how he had succeeded in fooling the guards on the Dieppe road in Paris. In spite of their serious mood, they laughed at the episode of the horse dung; then the evening ended with them having the confidence that Edouard would succeed in bringing his father and Annette into Sussex.

They waited a week for a message to come, but in that time, the cousins became re-acquainted and the countess received much support and friendship from Sir Thomas.

It amused Marianne to see Lucy and Edouard together; at first they were shy with one another, but by the end of the week, Marianne could see that there was no need on her part to proceed with any attempts at matchmaking. She did not leave the two of them on their own, but it was her custom to ride round the farms once a week and she did not want to neglect her duty because of their visitors.

So on that particular morning, Edouard and Lucy decided not to ride, but to have a walk as far as the small stone tower on the top of a hill at the edge of the Welford parkland; it had been erected to commemorate the battle of Blenheim in 1704 in which a local worthy had been killed.

On Edouard's second day in England, Sir Thomas had taken him to Brighton to be fitted out by his own tailor. By the end of the week, the one coat and breeches which Edouard had packed in his bag had been replaced by the latest in English fashion.

Lucy at his side was — in Edouard's eyes — very lovely in an overdress of deep blue worn with a shallow-crowned hat with curving brim which did not hide her dark curls.

It was a long walk to the tower, but they enjoyed the view from the top of the hill. Lucy was out of breath with the exertion and Edouard laughingly took her hand and encouraged her up the last slope.

They sat on the low wall which surrounded the tower.

'I am going to keep your hand in mine, Lucy,' Edouard told her.

'I suppose I should object,' she replied with a coquettish smile. 'But I am not going to. I will tell you about the view from here.'

'I don't want to hear about the view. I can see that we are looking back at Welford Grange and I would rather talk about you. But if you insist, what is the name of that village over there?'

'That is Ringmer. There is a well-known

English naturalist called the Reverend Gilbert White; he wrote a book about the natural history of his village of Selborne in Hampshire. It was published a few years ago and papa has it; the Reverend White lived at Delves House in Ringmer for a short time . . . '

Lucy stopped speaking as Edouard reached for her other hand and turned her to face him. 'Why are you telling me all this, Lucy Welford?'

She gave a grin. 'To stop you becoming familiar with me and holding both my hands.'

'I want to be familiar with you.'

'Edouard, that is a shocking thing to say to a young lady.'

'I don't think it is possible to shock you, Lucy. You love me as I love you.'

She pulled her hands away from him. 'How can you say such things and how do you know of my feelings for you?'

He laughed. 'My sweet girl, we fell in love the instant we met; you have told me so with every glance from those blue eyes and with every sweet word you have said to me. I love you very much, but that is all I can say. I cannot offer you marriage yet because I am an émigré in this country; I have to find my way.'

'Do you know what you are going to do,

Edouard?' she asked him.

'I know what I am going to try to do which is a different matter. We have a house in London; that is a good start and very wise of my father. I hope to find a post with *The Times* — I am fluent in both languages and I have studied at the Sorbonne. But, Lucy, it will be a little while before I can support a wife and at the moment, I cannot even begin to think of a betrothal. The most urgent thing is to bring Annette and my father over to England. You do understand that?'

Lucy had tears in her eyes. 'Yes, of course I do, your poor mama grieves so much. I hope that we will not have to wait many more days, it has been a week already and not a word from them.'

'I expect it is very difficult to send a message across the channel,' said Edouard seriously. 'I will wait two more days and if there is no news, I will ask your father to make arrangements for me to cross and bring them home.'

'But it is not safe for you to be in France, Edouard, you might be taken.' Lucy was fearful.

'I cannot consider myself, it is my father and Annette who are important. Do not worry, little one, it will all be achieved somehow. Now we must make our way back

68

to Welford Grange, it will be easier going downhill.' He put his hands to her shoulders. 'I cannot ask you to marry me yet, Lucy, but I am going to ask for a kiss . . . no, I am not, I am going to take it.'

And he brought her close to him and touched her soft young lips with his; the brief touch lingered into seconds and Lucy's face was flushed at her first kiss.

'I love you, Lucy,' he said.

'And I love you, Edouard,' said Lucy shyly in return.

★　★　★

Three days went by and no word had been received from France; neither Sir Thomas nor Edouard was surprised. The situation, however, did provoke a fierce quarrel between them.

After they had breakfasted, it was Sir Thomas's custom to retire to the library to attend to the affairs of his estate; or if he was not to be found there, he would be riding out, making sure that all was well at his farms; he did not have a steward and managed the estate himself.

On that morning, Edouard asked if he could speak to him privately.

'You are worrying about your father and

Annette,' Sir Thomas said on seeing the serious expression on the young vicomte's face.

'Yes, I must go, Cousin Thomas, I cannot leave it any longer. I believe that I can ask you to make the arrangements. Will M. and Mme Bézier accompany me again?'

Expecting trouble, Sir Thomas spoke very quietly. 'I am going to forbid you to go, Edouard.'

As had been expected, Edouard jumped to his feet in a rage. 'You cannot forbid me, sir, I must go. It is my duty.'

'Sit down, sit down, and listen to me, young man. Every second that you are on French soil, you are in danger. We do not know what has happened to your father, and you must think of your mama. She is already bereft at having to leave her husband and Annette behind; but she has you here with her and I think that your calming presence is helping her to keep her composure.'

'I don't believe it, Cousin. Mama would want me to go, she would think it my duty. I am sure of it. You cannot forbid it. I enjoy your hospitality and I am grateful for it, but I must be allowed to make up my own mind on this.'

Sir Thomas stood up. 'Very well, Edouard, I suggest you go and ask your mother. I think she will have left the breakfast-room by now.'

Edouard rushed out of the library to find the countess settling down in the drawing-room with Marianne and Lucy. It was a cold, wet morning and there was to be no riding.

'Mama.' Edouard burst in upon them and knelt down at his mother's knee. 'Our cousin is trying to forbid me from going to fetch my father and Annette from France. But I must go, who else is there? You want me to go, don't you, Mama? Please tell me you wish for it.'

There was a hush in the room. The countess went rigid and white; Marianne and Lucy held their breath. They could guess the outcome of Edouard's demand and were ready for it.

Even so, the scream which uttered from the lips of the countess startled them.

'Edouard . . . no, no . . . I will not have it. Do not ask it of me. Tell me it is not your intention, there must be someone else whom my cousin can send. Is it not bad enough not to have Maurice and Annette here without you disappearing as well? It is not safe, you know that it is not safe.'

All this was said in a high-pitched scream which at the same time was a wail of woe of a highly distressed woman.

Marianne rushed to her side, ready with

the hartshorn. 'Aunt Caroline, do not distress yourself. We will not let Edouard go, we will think of something. Lie back with the hartshorn and leave it all to us.' She stood up and faced Edouard who was standing grimly at their side.

'I *must* go, Marianne, surely you can see it. Who else can we ask?' he said angrily.

Marianne did not hesitate in her reply; she was at first angry and then thoughtful. 'How could you upset your mother in such a way? You might have known the effect it would have on her. Yes, someone must go and I will ask Harvey.'

Edouard stared. 'Harvey Burrage-Smith, your betrothed? But why should he go? He is not one of the family.'

'He will be one day and he knows how to go about things,' replied Marianne. 'He has been in London while Parliament has been sitting, but is back for a few days now. I will ride over to Broadoaks to see him this minute. Stay with your mother and reassure her that there is no need for you to go and that we will soon have your father and Annette in Sussex.'

# 4

Marianne hastily changed into her riding-dress and ran to the stables. She took no notice of the wind and the rain. Her beloved mare, Kirsty, was saddled for her and she was off across the park towards Sapstead. She loved to gallop and gave Kirsty her head; within ten minutes, she could see the village ahead and the red roofs of Broadoaks. The house was situated on the Welford Grange side of the village and had been well-named by Harvey's grandfather. A group of oak trees dominated the approach to the house and the drive was curved round them before it reached the front door.

As Marianne entered the gates, she saw a horseman moving along the drive towards the house, and in his elegant black riding jacket, she recognized Harvey. Deciding that in spite of the rain it would be easier to talk to him out of doors, she called his name, knowing that he would consider it unladylike.

'Harvey . . . Harvey, wait for me.'

Turning in the saddle, he saw her and he frowned; then thinking that he could hear a note of urgency in her voice, he trotted back to meet her. They came face to face under the shelter of one of the oak trees.

'What is it, Marianne, that you could not have waited until we had reached the house? And you are wet through.'

He is going to be starchy, thought Marianne. However am I going to ask him to go to France?

They had dismounted and stood close together under the tree; Marianne felt glad of the privacy it afforded.

'It is very urgent, Harvey, and I don't know how to ask you.' She thought she sounded foolish.

'Ask me what?'

'I will explain. We are in great trouble. I told you that my cousin, the Comte de Charnay and his daughter have not arrived from France and there is still no message from them. Edouard wants to go over and bring them back, but everything is against it. He would put himself in grave danger and my father forbids it. Edouard was going to defy my father and go, but Aunt Caroline had hysterics when she thought she might lose Edouard as well. She would only be comforted when I told her that I would come and ask you if you would go . . . ' She broke off as she saw a steely look come into his eyes.

'You did what?' He asked her the question

in such a way that she was almost afraid to repeat her words.

'I thought . . . ' she stammered. 'I had the idea that I could ask you to go over to France. I thought you would be willing to help us in our distress. Oh, I know you have Radical views, but sometimes humanitarianism comes first. A person's life is more important than a political tenet.'

'Are you daring to preach to me about my views, Marianne?'

'No, no, I am not. I just want you to be a kind person for once and go to France and rescue those who are dear to me. I am asking you to do it for me, for the Welfords. Never mind about the Revolution, there are rights and wrongs on both sides. How can you excuse this Reign of Terror? Think of the innocent people who have suffered and lost their lives at the guillotine. If we do not rescue them, my uncle and Annette will go to the guillotine, too.'

Mr Harvey Burrage-Smith was standing very stiffly, his mouth drawn in a straight line, his eyes hard.

'You ask the impossible,' he said clearly and icily.

'Are you refusing me, Harvey?'

'Of course I am refusing you; and what, might I ask, do you mean by asking me to be 'a kind person for once'. I consider that to be an insult. When have I been anything but kind to you?'

Marianne could feel a bitter anger rising in her, an anger against her betrothed because she knew that he was going to refuse her request.

'You are always polite, I will admit,' she muttered.

'Thank you. Now I will repeat that you are asking the impossible of me. You know my views and I will not go against the fight for liberty. Yes, I am a Whig and a Radical. I am a founding member of the London Revolution Society, our members have correspondence with workers throughout France. I will admit to you that your relatives might be innocent of most of the crimes and pretensions of the aristocracy, but lend my hand to help them, I will not.'

Marianne did lose her temper then. She stamped her foot and shouted at him.

'I hate you, I hate you. You are not human and I refuse to marry a monster. In fact, I refuse to marry you at all and you can have your ring; our betrothal is at an end. I believe in law and order — Liberty, Fraternity, Equality, too. But not at the expense of the lives of innocent people. Be careful that you are not fostering a revolution in your own country, Mr Harvey Burrage-Smith. Go back to your politician friends and I hope that I never have to see you again.'

Marianne did not know it, but at that moment she looked beautiful. In her haste, she had not worn a hat and her lovely auburn hair had come loose and had fallen about her shoulders. Her eyes were blazing, her breasts heaving under the damp and clinging wool cloth of her riding-dress.

Harvey did then what he had wanted to do for a long time, but the formality of their betrothal had prevented him. He pulled Marianne close to him until she strained to be free; her resistance only served to incense his intention and his lips were on hers, forcing them apart.

The shock of his embrace, the wild feelings of a passion she had never known before, forced Marianne to go limp in his arms. She returned his kiss with fervour.

Even as she did so, he let her go abruptly and she almost fell to the ground; he gave a bound and was on his horse and galloping furiously towards the house.

Marianne watched him, a shaking hand to her lips; there was only one question she could think to ask herself as she rode slowly home. Why did he never kiss me like that before, she kept thinking, and tears trickled down her cheeks; tears of hatred, tears of failure, and lastly, were they tears of love?

She was calmer by the time she reached Welford Grange and saying nothing to Lucy and her cousins, she sought out her father. He was still in the library.

'Papa,' said Marianne, as she stood quietly at his desk. 'I have been to ask Harvey to help us and he has refused. I lost my temper with him and our betrothal is at an end.'

Sir Thomas rose from his desk and they sat together by the fire. 'I am sorry, Marianne. I have always admired Harvey, but I do know of his political views. I suppose that your dear mama and I were wrong to arrange a marriage of convenience, though it seemed right at the time. Now, my dear, I will tell you that when Edouard came and told me that you had gone for Harvey, I did not think that you would succeed. So I have sent one of the stable boys off to Oxford with a message for Luke; he will lose his studies for a while, but I trust him to go to France for his cousins.'

Marianne felt a sense of relief. 'Did Edouard agree?' she asked her father.

Sir Thomas nodded. 'He still is not pleased, but he will let Luke go for the sake of his mother.' He looked at his eldest daughter. 'Marianne, I have something to ask of you, and I would not be asking you if I did not have every confidence that you could do it.'

'What are you saying, Papa?'

'Luke will do as I ask him, there is no question of that. He was a madcap when he was younger and although he has now become more studious, I think he will relish a rescue mission into France. But two questions arise. First of all, I do not think that Luke should go on his own; and the other thing is perhaps the more important. Annette is a young girl and I think she will need female company with her — '

'You mean . . . ' Marianne interrupted. She could guess what was coming and felt a stir of excitement.

'Yes, you have guessed. I am going to ask you if you be willing to accompany Luke and to bring Annette here.'

The passage of arms with Harvey Burrage-Smith was instantly forgotten and Marianne was enthusiastic. 'But of course I will go, Papa, there is no question. You must tell me your plans. Do you wish us to go disguised? And don't forget that neither of us speaks very good French; only what we learned from Biddy years ago. Though, of course, Luke did travel the continent before he went up to Oxford, so he will be more fluent in French than I am.'

'I have thought and thought about the best

way to go about it,' said her father. 'The only conclusion I can come to is to leave the final arrangements to M. and Mme Bézier, for I have every confidence in them. I understand that they have helped several noble families escape into England. They seem an odd couple and I believe Mme Bézier to be the brains behind it all.'

'Edouard said that M. Bézier hardly said a word,' remarked Marianne, 'though I believe he speaks English very well, so she leaves all the talking to him when they are over here. I suppose that they must complement each other.' She looked at the serious face of her father. 'How do you get in touch with them, Papa? Do you have an intermediary over here?'

He nodded. 'Yes, I suppose it is safe to tell you, though I know very little about it myself; it is all done in great secrecy as you might imagine. This will surprise you, Marianne, and you must promise to keep the confidence closely to yourself. Tell no one. When I needed help to have our cousins brought here, I received a message sent from France to tell me that all arrangements were to be made through Jack Findon. He is a Sussex man and works as an under-gardener to your Harvey.'

Marianne looked astonished and could

only mutter, 'He is not my Harvey.'

'I know, dear, I will put it another way. He is the under-gardener at Broadoaks.'

'I cannot believe it. Do you mean to say that although Harvey is a Republican and supports the Revolution and also refuses to help us, that all the time, one of his employees is helping to bring the émigrés to England? It cannot be true, Papa.'

He gave a little laugh. 'I can only tell you the truth of what happened when the de Charnays were brought out of Paris. It was Jack Findon who arranged it all — I am not allowed to know how — and it was M. and Mme Bézier who carried out the exercise. One of the boys goes with a message and I meet Jack secretly at night. I am not going to tell you about that . . . why are you laughing, Marianne? It is a very serious matter.'

'It amuses me that Harvey is being hoodwinked. It is a case of just deserts for refusing to help us. I hope he stays in London for a long time; I have no wish to meet him again.'

'We cannot ignore him completely, Marianne. He is our nearest neighbour.'

'Well, fortunately he is not in Sussex very often and if he calls, I will be out riding. I hope I never have to speak to him again.' She rose and gave her father a kiss on the cheek.

'Thank you for explaining to me, Papa. Now we must look forward to Luke's arrival and you will be able to give us your instructions.'

Marianne went into the drawing-room and told them of Harvey's refusal to help and of Luke's expected arrival. She looked fearfully at Edouard and was pleased to see that he took the news well.

'So be it!' he said. 'I understand now that Mama needs me and it would only endanger Papa's and Annette's chances if I was to go to Neufchâtel. It is hard for me, but it is for the best. I will go and apologize to Cousin Thomas for my outburst.'

The countess recovered her spirits when she heard that Edouard was not going to leave her and that there was a chance that in three of four days, the family might be all together again.

Marianne and Lucy walked out in the afternoon and had a lot to talk about; by bedtime, Marianne felt tired. She had recovered from her fury at Harvey and did not regret breaking off the betrothal; but on retiring, she found that sleep eluded her as she remembered the force and passion of Harvey's kiss. She drifted into sleep wishing that she had known that particular Harvey Burrage-Smith before; a man of passion and not just a civil parliamentarian.

★ ★ ★

Luke arrived at Welford Grange in the middle of the following morning, having set off from Oxford in his gig at daybreak and driven fast and foolishly on poor but quiet roads. On his arrival, he refused refreshment, telling his family that he had stopped at Basingstoke to partake of a hearty breakfast.

Luke was nineteen years of age and was the tallest member of the Welford family; his build was thin but athletic, his looks no more than ordinary. He was an even-tempered young man with a ready smile and a kindly manner. His sisters loved him.

He greeted them all in the drawing-room, accepted coffee, then went in search of his father. Not finding him in the library, Luke walked to the stables and learned that his father had ridden out soon after breakfast and had said that he would not be away for any great length of time.

Luke had no idea why he had been called home on a matter of 'great urgency' as the note had said and his sisters and Edouard refused to discuss the matter before he had seen his father. He learned enough, however, to discover that only the countess and Edouard had arrived from France; it did not take a lot of imagination to assume that

83

someone had to go across the channel to bring Annette and her father to England. He remembered his cousin, the count, very well and had an idea that Edouard's young sister had been no more than a plain little schoolgirl on their last visit.

He returned to the library and looked at his father's copy of the poems of John Donne, Andrew Marvell and the metaphysical poets of the seventeenth century; he had become unexpectedly interested in their verse as part of his university studies.

He did not have to wait long for his father's return; Sir Thomas came into the library before the morning was over and looked pleased to see his son. They shook hands.

'Luke, it is good of you to come so quickly. I saw your horse in the stables and I imagine that you travelled in your gig. Let me pour you some wine and I will tell you why I need you so urgently. I could not put it all in a note, and in any case, it was not safe to commit to paper.'

'You made it sound mysterious, Father. Is it to do with our French cousins? I understand that only Edouard and his mother have arrived.'

'Yes, that is so,' Sir Thomas replied. 'Everything went according to plan and they left Paris without any trouble. But on the way to Dieppe, little Annette became ill of a fever; they stopped at a small town called Neufchâtel and a lodging was found for Annette and her father. Cousin Caroline and Edouard came on to England as planned, but we have had no word from France. It is very worrying. We do not even know if they are still alive; someone must go for them.'

'You want me to go?' asked Luke in a very calm tone.

'Yes, I have brought you home to ask if you would be willing. Edouard badly wanted to go, but his mother was too upset at the idea and it would have been foolish to have had the Comte and the Vicomte d'Amand both trying to escape. Are you willing, Luke?' Sir Thomas knew what his son's answer would be.

Luke grinned. 'You knew that I would be very pleased to go. Will I be on my own and how do I cross? Then I have to get from the coast to . . . Neufchâtel, did you say it was?'

'One question at a time. No, you will not be on your own. Annette is a young girl, she has been ill and she will need some feminine company. Marianne will go with you.'

'Marianne? Goodness gracious, I thought you would send a maid.'

'No,' replied his father. 'I thought it over carefully, and I have asked Marianne; she is prepared to go. It is not yet known if you will travel in disguise.'

Luke frowned. 'Is it wise to be dressed as the son and daughter of an English landowner? And you have not told me what transport we will have in France.'

'Wait, wait, all in good time. I will tell you how the de Charnay family came out of Paris. They dressed as peasants and a wagon arrived at their home in Auteuil to take them to the yacht which was waiting for them just outside Dieppe. I told you why the escape did not succeed completely.'

'Who was driving the wagon? Was it a daring English gentleman in disguise?'

Sir Thomas laughed. 'You have been listening to too many stories of the French aristocracy escaping to England. No, the wagon was driven by a French couple, a M. and Mme Bézier; they are country people and come from the south, so they are under no suspicion. Mme Bézier was the spokeswoman for the two of them and she was also the driver of the wagon. It seems she is quite a character. You must persuade Edouard to tell you of their ruse for getting them out of France; it was most ingenious and failed only because of Annette's illness.'

'But where are these Béziers now?' asked Luke. 'And how do they get their orders?'

Sir Thomas frowned. 'You have asked me questions which I cannot answer. As you can imagine, all this is done in the greatest secrecy and I have to act through a local contact. Marianne knows who it is, but I will tell no one else. I have seen my contact this morning and have been told that M. and Mme Bézier are still somewhere in this country awaiting the instruction to go back to Neufchâtel to fetch the other members of the de Charnay family. They will be sought out today, and tomorrow, we should receive our orders. Are you satisfied, Luke? Are there any other questions?'

Luke was thoughtful. 'No, I don't think so. I will have to wait; it will be difficult to have patience.'

Sir Thomas smiled. 'The time will pass quickly enough. Off you go and speak to our cousins. Let them know that Annette and her father will be safe in your hands.'

Luke was told the story of the coffin and they all laughed; even the countess who seemed reassured now that she knew some action was being taken to bring her husband and her daughter to England.

Sir Thomas was missing again after dinner that evening and as soon as he returned, he called Luke and Marianne to the library.

Edouard stayed with his mother and spoke softly with Lucy.

'I have a lot to tell the two of you,' Sir Thomas said, 'so please listen carefully. My contact has seen M. and Mme Bézier and Madame has laid the plan. She and M. Bézier will go with the two of you to France tomorrow; the *Marie Rose* will sail at 8 a.m. from Newhaven, so we will have to make a very early start to meet them there. I will come with you in the carriage.'

'Has she told us what we should wear?' asked Marianne.

'Yes, yes, have patience. The Béziers wish you to go as their son and his sweetheart. There is the guard at Dieppe to consider and it is possible that he will remember the wagon going through to St Pierre ten days ago. Mme Bézier is rather a distinctive figure, I think you will agree. So she asks that you, Luke, should wear the same clothes as Edouard was wearing on that day — if he still has them, that is. He was dressed as a French peasant if I remember rightly . . . what is it, Luke? You are frowning.'

'I am a lot taller than Edouard, I doubt his clothes will fit me.'

'We will make do somehow. You will be sitting in the back of the wagon with Marianne, I imagine, and I trust that the wagon will soon slip past the guard. Then straight on to Neufchâtel to fetch the count and Annette. You will return the same day, all being well.'

'But the guard at Dieppe will notice that we have extra passengers on our return,' objected Luke.

'You can leave such explanations to Mme Bézier, she will have some kind of story ready. I think we can be sure of that!' Sir Thomas turned to Marianne. 'My dear girl, I want you to find one of the maid's dresses and a shawl. A pretty dress if you can find it, low in the bodice, a little *risqué* if you understand my meaning. And wear your hair loose in a careless fashion.'

Marianne smiled. 'I think I can manage that, Papa, it will be quite an adventure.'

'It is not without its dangers for France is quite an ugly place at the moment. But I trust the two of you and know that you will do your best for your cousins. Off you go now. You must have your clothing ready for a very early start in the morning. I will go and tell Caroline and Edouard what is happening.'

At six o'clock the next morning, it was still dark. It was also very cold.

Marianne had sought out Janey, the parlour maid, who was the same height and build as herself and between them, they had found a suitable dress for the trip to France. Janey was not the owner of many dresses, but was pleased to exchange a thick woollen dress of a bright orange colour for one of Marianne's fine muslin afternoon dresses.

The colour of the dress against Marianne's hair was startling, but the skirt was full and warm, the sleeves long, the bodice low in the neck and tight fitting. Both girls laughed when Marianne tried it on. Fortunately the thick shawl which Janey found was a dark brown and most of the lurid colour of the dress was hidden.

Luke, wearing Edouard's farm clothes, was slightly unhappy because the breeches barely reached his ankles; but Marianne made him pull his thick stockings over the breeches and they went out to the carriage with the feeling that they looked the parts they were supposed to be playing.

It was light by the time they reached Newhaven and they found the Béziers waiting for them on the small harbour; the fishing boats had left long since. The rowing boat was ready and they could see the *Marie Rose* close by.

It was easy to recognize Mme Bézier from Edouard's description for she was dressed in the same black and with the same preposterous bonnet. Marianne caught a glimpse of weathered brown skin about the mouth and chin and that was all. M. Bézier was standing quietly at her side, but he greeted them politely in English and helped Marianne into the rowing boat.

On the *Marie Rose*, they all leant over the rail watching for a glimpse of the French coast. It was Marianne's first trip across the channel, though she had been taken as a child along the coast from Newhaven to Brighthelmstone.

It was as they were setting off that Mme Bézier told them what to expect. She had given what Marianne could only describe as a cackle when she was shown the borrowed dress.

'Very indiscreet, Miss Marianne, and just what I wanted.'

Then she continued with her instructions, talking very quickly in French which the two of them could just about follow and with the same high-pitched crack in her voice which Annette had noticed.

But the old woman knew exactly what she was about. 'This is not a pleasure trip, my dears, we must have our wits about us. We have our wagon waiting for us at St Pierre-sur-Mer, we are well known in that little place, Bézier and myself. In the wagon, you will find some empty crates; they were filled with poultry when we left Dieppe, now they must return empty. You can sit on them or lean against them, whichever you wish, as long as you can manage to pretend that you are sweethearts. Don't forget that when we came from Dieppe, you were your cousin Edouard, Mr Luke, and that you had a bottle of cognac in your hand. You were also very drunk and you offered some of the drink to the guard, I think he will remember. But now you have your sweetheart with you and you must behave yourself! I know that Miss Marianne is your sister, but you can make a pretence, can you not?'

'I will be sure to try, Mme Bézier,' said Luke. 'Is it very far to Dieppe?'

'Two or three miles, but it is not the distance that worries me, it is the guard. You must listen very carefully to what I say to him. I shall tell him that we are driving to Neufchâtel to fetch my brother and his young daughter. Then we are going straight back to our friends in St Pierre-sur-Mer. Miss Marianne, I shall pretend that you are from St Pierre and that all the family will be there to celebrate your betrothal to Mr Luke. You will play your part?'

Marianne nodded. 'Yes, of course I will. It sounds quite easy, but we realize that you have to be very clever to deceive the guards. I don't suppose it is as difficult in Dieppe as it is in Paris.'

Mme Bézier nodded. 'You are quite right. In Paris, the guards are in uniform and they are armed. There are many of them, too, especially at the North Gate. We try and avoid the North Gate if possible; if anyone is caught there, it is straight to the guillotine. A French aristocrat is guilty not only of his avoidance of the taxes and his noble lifestyle when people cannot afford to buy bread; he also becomes guilty if he tries to escape from his country.'

Luke joined in. 'So you are sympathizing with the aristocracy, Mme Bézier?'

'Young man, I sympathize with some of them. A lot of noble gentlemen are good to their farm workers and make sure that they are properly housed and fed; but for every one of those, there are the wicked ones who think only of their own riches, and their welfare and comfort. They are against the Revolution. But, you see, the Committee of Public Safety, and M. Robespierre in particular, do not distinguish between the two. If you are of noble family, it is the guillotine.'

'So you help those families who merit it to escape to England?' he said to her thoughtfully.

'We do. There are those in England who condemn the Revolution. Your Mr Burke and his followers, for example; he has published in his book *Reflections on the Revolution* his ideas on the subject. He sees evil in the outbreak of the mob against the rule of law and order; he even called the mob the 'swinish multitude'. His book created a great stir in England; a lot of people supported him, including King George and many of the sovereigns of Europe. But I go on, *mes enfants*, it is a favourite topic of mine and I do what I can to bring the innocent to peaceful England.'

Marianne was reminded of Harvey. 'But, Mme Bézier, not all of England takes the same view. I know of someone — and he is a Member of Parliament, too — who sides with the Revolution and has encouraged others to support him.'

'Mademoiselle, in all things, there are two sides; no two people think alike about some things, particularly when it comes to politics.'

'You are very wise, Mme Bézier,' commented Marianne and wondered what M. Bézier thought. He had not said a word throughout the exchange but she noticed that he nodded his head from time to time.

'Ha-ha,' came the cackle from madame. 'It is common sense, no more, and having your wits about you, of course. And now we must certainly have our wits about us because soon we will see the coast of France.'

Half an hour later, the rowing boat was on its way out from St Pierre-sur-Mer to take them off the *Marie Rose.*

Marianne and Luke stepped ashore to find themselves in a small fishing village which was not even big enough to have a harbour; there was just a slipway for the fishing boats.

A row of sturdy cottages lined the shore; behind these were the bigger houses of those who lived between Paris and the coast and who liked to spend their time riding along the sands, and fishing, and enjoying the fresh breeze which blew across the channel.

At one of the larger cottages, Marianne and Luke were taken in to meet the Bézier's friends, M. and Mme Franchot, and they all sat round the kitchen table to a breakfast of small pieces of fried fish with plenty of home-baked bread and tankards of ale. There is no shortage of food in a French fishing village, Marianne was thinking as she enjoyed the welcome meal.

Mme Bézier was in a hurry to be off and they had hardly the time to leave the breakfast table before she was asking M. Franchot to bring the wagon round to the front of the cottage.

It was kept on wasteland at the rear of the cottages and M. Franchot busied himself harnessing the horse and helping them all into the wagon. Marianne had expected M. Bézier to drive, but now that she was getting to know the old lady, it seemed natural that it was madame who took the reins.

Luke and Marianne climbed into the back and sat down with their backs to the empty crates; Luke had his arm round Marianne's shoulders and his cheek rested on her soft hair. It was a truly brotherly gesture, but anyone seeing them would easily have taken them for young lovers.

The track along the cliff towards Dieppe was very stony and uneven, but bumps and jolts were the least of their troubles. Neither of them knew what was going to happen when they reached the guard at Dieppe and the short journey passed very tensely and silently.

It did not seem very long before they heard Mme Bézier's loud cry.

'Mr Luke, the guard is in his place and I can see quite clearly that it is the same one. If you do have to speak, say only a few words so that he cannot suspect that you are not French, then turn your attention to Miss Marianne. And do not worry, we will succeed.'

They stopped at the entrance to the town and as before, they found only the one guard there.

He smiled broadly when he recognized the wagon and M. and Mme Bézier.

'*Bonjour*, madame. I remember you, I hope you enjoyed your stay with your relatives in St Pierre. I also remember your son, he had drunk too much of the brandy, but he kindly offered me a swig. Now I can see that he has other consolations! And what is the name of your sweetheart, monsieur?' He addressed himself to Luke.

'Marianne,' was all Luke had to say and thankfully buried his face in Marianne's long hair.

'Where do you go, madame?' The guard turned back to Mme Bézier who spoke quickly and in her usual patois.

'We go to Neufchâtel to fetch my brother and his daughter; the family is having a party in St Pierre to celebrate the betrothal of my son and Marianne. She is a pretty girl, is she not? Her home is in St Pierre and all the family are gathering in her house for the celebration. It will be a very happy occasion.'

The guard nodded, but frowned as though there was something which was bothering him.

'And the madame who was with you

before? I seem to remember that she was very pale and did not look well, she sat between you and your husband on the driving seat, did she not? I had thought her to be the mother of the young monsieur, but perhaps I was mistaken. I trust that she has recovered.'

None of them had expected the dozy guard to remember such a thing and to ask after the countess. Marianne held her breath and felt Luke's hand on the shoulder tighten. How would Mme Bézier wriggle out of this one, she thought?

But she soon discovered that Mme Bézier was equal to anything.

'Yes, you are quite right in thinking that the lady was Marianne's mother; the whole family had been visiting their cousins near Dieppe and poor Mme Benaud became ill and did not return to St Pierre with the rest of the family. We brought her back when we next visited in that area, and yes, she did still look pale. Your are quite right, it was very observant of you. Now she is at home and making a good recovery.'

Marianne squeezed Luke's hand; she had never heard such a weak story — surely the guard will never believe it, she thought.

And she was quite right. The guard scratched his head and frowned.

'I do not think it will do,' he said. 'I don't

know why they post me here, but we must be vigilant; I say to myself, why would the émigrés try to leave for England by way of Dieppe when Calais is so near and the crossing is so much shorter. There is fear and bloodshed in the country, it is everywhere, even in a quiet place like this. No, madame, it is not satisfactory, your story; and then there is the problem of why you drive the wagon and not your husband. I think you must explain to my superior officer, I will fetch him.'

Mme Bézier did not move except to give a slight nod of the head. 'Very well,' she said. 'Perhaps I can make him understand; be pleased to fetch him quickly for we are expected in Neufchâtel.'

The guard walked to a small building along the street, coming out again very quickly followed by a short, stout man in the uniform of a police officer.

'This is M. Genet,' said the guard. 'Please explain your story to him, even if it means giving him all the details of your family. He will listen carefully, so leave nothing out.'

Marianne watched as Mme Bézier talked to the officer; she did not get down from her perch on the wagon, but leaned over to speak to him. It was a torrent of French which neither Marianne, nor Luke could understand. They just watched and kept a tight hold on each other, thinking they had met with disaster right at the start of their mission. The officer was nodding, and then to their surprise, they saw Mme Bézier pick up her husband's arm. They saw that the arm was quite limp, it looked useless and certainly could not have held the reins of the horse.

'She is explaining why M. Bézier does not drive and we know very well that he has two quite good arms for he helped you into the rowing boat at Newhaven, Marianne,' said Luke in a whisper.

'Shhhh,' was all Marianne said in reply and no more was said between them; they simply watched silent and helpless as the little scene was enacted before them. Then came the surprise as they saw Mme Bézier put her hand into the pocket of her very full skirts and bring out a small leather bag which obviously held a quantity of louis for she shook it in front of the officer and his guard.

The officer took it from her, clicked his heels and walked back into his office.

Mme Bézier quickly took up the reins, nodded to the guard, and they drove out of Dieppe.

As soon as they were clear of the town, she pulled up at the side of a rather muddy road, and turned to Marianne and Luke.

'My children, are you well? We had a little

difficulty there, but you will soon learn that in our country a guard can usually be bribed. It is wise to carry a little bag of louis in case of emergency. And that nearly was an emergency, was it not? I had not expected trouble from that guard, he has always seemed very lazy and not at all on the alert. However, I was mistaken, and we have managed to get ourselves out of the trouble. It must be hoped that it will be a different guard on our return or I will need another little bag of louis.'

Marianne and Luke smiled bleakly, Mme Bézier cracked her whip and they were off again.

They made good progress in spite of the poor condition of the road and the hold-up in Dieppe and entered Neufchâtel by mid-morning. Mme Bézier drove straight into the yard at Le Coq d'Or and told Luke and Marianne to go into the inn while she waited.

'Be as quick as you can,' she said to them and for a moment she seemed to have lost some of her cheeriness.

Brother and sister hurried into the inn and Luke, in his better French, asked for M. de Charnay and his daughter.

The landlord raised his hands in horror.

'Monsieur, mademoiselle, it was yesterday. They have taken M. de Charnay to the lock-up, and the poor little Annette is locked on her own in her room. She cries and cries, *la petite*; if you have come for her, go up to her quickly for we fear the worst for her father.'

# 5

Marianne felt as though she had been struck dumb; she was glad of Luke's strong hand on her arm.

'Take us to her please. Do you have the key?'

'But yes, they trust me. I will take you.'

The inn was cold and dark, but it was not shabby. They climbed steep, narrow stairs on to a dim landing and the landlord led them to a door at the end of the passage.

As he opened the door, he spoke in a loud whisper. 'Mlle Annette, do not worry, it is your cousins from England.'

Marianne heard a loud shriek and they entered the room to find Annette standing by the bed, her hands outstretched, tears streaming down her face.

'It is Luke,' she cried out and threw herself into his arms. He held her tight and met Marianne's worried eyes across the dark head. 'You have come and it is too late,' Annette sobbed.

Then she lifted her head and saw Marianne. 'It is my dearest Marianne, whatever shall we do?'

'Sit down with us on the bed and tell us what has happened,' said Marianne gently. 'But as quickly as you can, Annette, for the wagon is waiting for us in the yard.'

Annette was stammering in her haste and excitement. 'You will know that I was ill and Papa stayed with me? The landlord and his wife have been very kind ... but I must hurry. I did get better but we had no way of sending a message. We did not worry at first because I was sure that Edouard would come. Where is Edouard? Oh, never mind, I must tell you about poor Papa. He was in this very room and talking to me kindly and he had forgotten to use his peasant voice, he was talking as the count. The door burst open and there were two soldiers and they asked him if he was Le Comte de Charnay. He denied it, but they said that they had their suspicions and now they had heard him speak in his own voice. It was to be the town lock-up for him until they received their instructions from Paris. 'My daughter,' said Papa. He was very composed, but he looked white and old. I was crying, but they took no notice and said that I was to stay in my room and on my own. I have had a good woman with me while I was ill — Marie is her name — but she was not to be allowed in. The landlord would bring me my food. Luke, Marianne, what are we to do?

Oh, poor Papa, they will take him to the guillotine.'

Annette sobbed again and Marianne put an arm around her, looking over her head to Luke. 'Go and ask Mme Bézier what we should do. How can we rescue my cousin from the lock-up? Hurry, Luke, we are in great danger — though it is odd, I feel quite calm.'

Luke ran down the stairs and out to the yard. Mme Bézier was still sitting on the wagon as though she was poised to be off. She frowned when she saw that Luke was on his own.

'What is it?' she asked briskly.

'It is terrible, Mme Bézier. The count is in the lock-up and they threaten to take him back to Paris. Annette has recovered from her illness, but she is very upset. She is locked in her room, but the landlord let us in. What shall we do?'

There was an awful silence in the courtyard of the inn; the only sound which Luke could hear was the shuffling of the horses in the stables.

Then it was M. Bézier who spoke in a very quiet voice. Luke had not heard him utter a single sound until that moment. 'My wife will advise you, she will know what to do.'

But Luke could see that Mme Bézier was

hesitating; when she spoke, it was sharply. 'We must go back to St Pierre, it is imperative to get Annette away from Neufchâtel as quickly as possible.'

'But her father?' interrupted Luke.

'I will think. Annette will not want to come, but tell her that I will think of something. She can rely on Mme Bézier. Go quickly.'

Back in the bedroom, Luke found Annette a little calmer, but this was soon undone.

'What did Mme Bézier say?' asked Marianne. She was holding Annette's hand.

'We must get Annette to St Pierre as quickly as possible.'

'No, no, I will not go, I will not leave Papa. How can you think that I will leave him?' It was almost a scream which came from Annette. She clutched at Marianne who was looking grim and frightened.

Luke went up to Annette and touched her wet cheek. 'Be brave, Annette, we must have confidence in Mme Bézier. From what I have heard of her, things don't go wrong when they are in her hands. Look how she managed to bring you out of Paris with Edouard in a coffin.'

It was not a time to make light of anything, but the memory of the safe journey from their home, seemed to calm Annette.

'Very well,' she said. 'I will go to St Pierre-sur-Mer for safety, but I will not leave France without Papa. And why has Edouard not come?'

'It is too complicated to tell you now, the Béziers are waiting. Have you a bag?'

'Yes, it has been ready for days, for we hoped that someone would come.'

When the three of them reached the yard, having thanked the landlord and been told that everything was paid for, they found that Mme Bézier had got down from the wagon. She put her hands to Annette's shoulders. 'We meet again, little one. Do not fear, leave it all to me. Now climb up into the wagon with your cousins, we must hurry.'

Dieppe was soon reached and the guard greeted them cheerily, remembering his share of the louis; the wagon hardly came to a halt. 'You are quick,' he said as he waved them through. 'And where is monsieur?'

Mme Bézier was ready for the question. 'He suffers from the gout and did not feel in the mood for merrymaking, so we leave him behind.'

Inside the Franchot's cottage once again, they were given hot drinks. Mme Bézier joined them and then went outside with her husband; they obviously needed to discuss the next steps to take.

Annette would say nothing except that she refused to leave France without her father, but Luke felt certain that Mme Bézier would want them to return to England and he sat with Annette's hand in his and tried to speak to her kindly and patiently.

At last, the French couple returned and as usual, madame was the spokeswoman.

'My children,' she said, looking at the three of them and at Annette in particular. 'There is no need to tell you that we are in serious trouble, but we must try and look at things in a way which is positive. First of all, the *Marie Rose* waits to take us back to England and it is dangerous for her to be seen for a long time in St Pierre. Already she has sailed along the coast as far as Fécamp and back, I have spoken with her captain. He is anxious to be gone.'

'But what about Papa?' cried Annette.

'*Ma petite*,' said Mme Bézier, going up to the young girl, 'I can think of only one thing to do to secure your father's safe release. It needs an English gentleman to plead his cause and I believe that Sir Thomas Welford will be willing to help his cousin.'

Marianne looked at Luke and they both had doubt in their expressions.

'What can my father do?' asked Luke.

'I cannot be sure,' came the reply. 'But I

will speak with him and try to explain to him the way things are going in France. It is my country and I am ashamed of the violence and the bloodshed. Now our queen has gone, too, and who do we have to rule us? Will it be that Danton or that Robespierre? Bah, it is too awful to contemplate.'

'So you will cross in the *Marie Rose* and seek out my father?' The question came from Marianne this time.

'We will all go,' replied the Frenchwoman. 'It will mean, at least, that Annette will be safely with her mother.'

'*Non, non*,' cried out Annette. 'I will not go, I will not leave my father here in jail. I cannot do it and you cannot make me. Take Luke and Marianne if you wish. I will wait here in St Pierre until my cousin, Sir Thomas, comes and secures Papa's release.'

There followed ten minutes of fierce argument, with Annette crying and shouting and Mme Bézier beginning to lose her patience. But she gave in at last.

'Very well, you all stay here. I will ask Mme Franchot. I will not leave Annette on her own. We will be gone for only one night if all goes well and I will bring Sir Thomas tomorrow morning. Take care, and do not venture out. There is danger everywhere. Come, Gaston.'

The pair left the cottage and from the window, the three young people saw them get into the rowing boat, then very quickly board the *Marie Rose*. They set off without delay.

The day passed slowly for Marianne, Luke and Annette, but Marianne had the amusement of watching Luke being very protective towards Annette and the young girl ending the day looking adoringly at him. Marianne mused: Edouard and Lucy, and now Luke and Annette, it seemed that romance had lifted the sombre mood of the cousins.

Next morning, they were at the cottage window as soon as it became light, straining their eyes for a sight of the *Marie Rose*. A fisherman sat in the rowing boat; he was on the watch-out, too.

The white sails came into view at last.

'It is here,' called out Annette. 'Oh, I do hope my cousin has come. I cannot bear it.'

Luke put a hand on her shoulder and they all watched.

The rowing boat put out and when it reached the *Marie Rose*, part of the enigma of the next few minutes began and had the three of them in the cottage mystified.

First of all, a tall younger gentleman stepped into the boat, followed by an older man of a much broader build; Marianne imagined this to be her father yet thought she

110

would have recognized him more distinctly.

There was no sign of Mme Bézier, nor was her husband to be seen, unless he had suddenly transformed himself from peasant to gentleman. There was something familiar about the younger man, Marianne muttered to Luke who was silent with his own thoughts.

The gentlemen stepped from the rowing boat and started walking towards them, M. Franchot having gone to meet them.

Marianne held her breath, it can't be . . . it's not possible . . . don't be silly, she was telling herself.

The door of the cottage opened and into the living room stepped Mr Harvey Burrage-Smith.

He was followed by the younger man whom, Marianne could now see, was dressed in servant's livery.

Mr Harvey Burrage-Smith was magnificent; dark hair unpowdered and swept thickly back, brilliant white neck cloth under a superbly cut tail-coat of deep crimson and worn over grey breeches and stockings.

He looked around him with a smile and Marianne could bear it no longer.

'Harvey, what are you doing here? Why have you come? We were expecting Papa.'

'I have been summoned to help you,

Marianne,' he said coolly.

'But who is this with you? And where is Mme Bézier? And M. Bézier is missing, too. Are they still on the *Marie Rose*?'

'No, they are not. I could not tolerate your Mme Bézier, she talks too much and would be of little use to me in my mission. I have brought Desmond; he is my coachman and my valet, whom you have probably met before. I go nowhere without him. Are you not pleased to see me?'

That is why I was thinking that the other man seemed familiar, thought Marianne, but what does Harvey think he is doing? She was not in the least polite when she answered his question. 'No, I am not pleased to see you. In the first place, we have quarrelled, and then I was expecting Papa who is to go and rescue Annette's father . . . oh, you have not met Annette.' Marianne turned to the young girl who looked both upset and puzzled. 'Annette, allow me to introduce Mr Harvey Burrage-Smith. Do you remember him from the last time you visited us? He is our nearest neighbour in Sussex. I was betrothed to him, but he refused to come to Paris to your rescue and we quarrelled. We are no longer betrothed and I cannot imagine what he is doing here; he is in favour of the Revolution. Harvey, this is Annette de Charnay, our little cousin; she is never far from Luke's side and I think she is about to fall in love with him . . . I am sorry, I go on. You have taken me by surprise.'

Harvey took no notice of her and bent over Annette's hand. 'I am pleased to meet you again; you were quite a little girl on your last visit. I will call you Annette. I am sorry that you have been ill and I am sorry that your father has been taken. Take no notice of Marianne, I will do my best for you.' He turned to Luke. 'Luke, I am glad to see that you are here to keep the young ladies in order!' Harvey and Luke were old friends.

Marianne persisted in her questioning. 'What are you going to do, Harvey? You won't betray the count, will you?'

She saw Harvey stiffen and she thought that she had gone too far; there was a lot here she did not understand. This was a different Harvey again.

'If we can be private,' he replied. 'I will tell you of my plans. Where is the wagon which brought the de Charnays here? And where can I obtain a carriage? Desmond, stay here and amuse the young people.'

Marianne could feel herself getting deeper and deeper into a tangle of deceptions, disasters and emotions. When Harvey had come into the room, her heart had given an unruly bound, yet she felt that he was playing some devious kind of game. She took him round to the back of the cottage thankfully, hoping that he would be able to dispel her misgivings.

They stood together at the side of the wagon and Harvey looked perplexed. 'This is the vehicle which Mme Bézier used to bring your cousins out of Paris? Good God, I think her talkative ways must hide a courageous and crafty nature. What did you make of her, Marianne?'

Why is he talking about Mme Bézier, she wondered? 'They were an ill-assorted pair, but they worked well together. She was never at a loss and could not get back to England soon enough to fetch my father. Why have you come, Harvey? I don't understand anything.'

'I will tell you as quickly as I can. Mme Bézier went to your father, but he did not feel equal to coming over to France. He rode over to see me straight away and asked if I would come.'

'But, Harvey, you know what your views are. I do, too. That is why we quarrelled. Why have you suddenly changed? Do you really propose to go to Neufchâtel to try to free the count?'

'If you knew me better, my dear Marianne,

you would learn that politics are very complicated; things are not always as they seem. But yes, I am in favour of Liberty, Equality, Fraternity as the cry is. I believe that many of the aristocracy in France are both corrupt and cruel — '

'But so is Robespierre cruel,' she interrupted harshly.

'Be quiet and listen to me. After our quarrel, I went back to my duties in London and at Westminster, I made a few discreet enquiries about the Comte de Charnay. What I found out was interesting and made me feel sorry that I had not agreed to help you. Are you listening?'

'Yes.'

'Very well. It appears that your cousin had a considerable amount of money lodged in London and had bought a property; he also had an English wife. He sincerely believed that life in France under Louis XVI had been wrong, the peasants were badly treated even though he, himself, had been good to those who worked for him. He sided with the bourgoisie to try and bring about a better France. But as with many others of his class, he was the object of hatred and suspicion and the mob ruled, as you know. It was his plan to try and come to London, and to lie low until the Terror was over — he could see that the end was in sight — then return to try and bring law and order to his country. I believe that you once told me that you believed in law and order, my sweet.'

Marianne stamped her foot. 'I am *not* your sweet. And you have told me all this and it still does not explain why it is you who have come to rescue my cousin.'

'It is easy, my love. If you were in England and heeding what your father is reading in the newspapers, you would learn that there is already war between England and France. And our Foreign Office is very interested in the Comte de Charnay. When they learned of his imprisonment, they turned to me to go and rescue him.'

Marianne was becoming lost. 'But, Harvey, why should they ask you of all people?'

He laughed at her. 'It is simple; they know of my activities in the London Revolution Society. I am known to be on the side of the Revolution. They think that I will have no trouble in persuading his captors to release the count. I will make sure that they do not ask where his family is or that I am taking him to England.' He looked at her. 'Why do you frown?'

Marianne sighed. 'It is all so complicated, but I must think only of Annette and my cousin. That is why you are here even if I

116

cannot understand a word of it; a 'cock and bull' story I think you might call it.'

'There is no need to be vulgar, Marianne,' he remarked stiffly. 'Let us forget the rights and wrongs of it and concentrate on getting to the count. I have wasted enough time already, but I had a particular motive for wanting you to know of my reason for coming.'

'Am I to know what that reason is?' she asked curiously.

'No, not at the moment. Perhaps one day. Now I want you to tell me exactly where the count is imprisoned, and how it came about.'

Marianne was glad to concentrate on the issue of her cousin's imprisonment. 'They had got as far as a small town called Neufchâtel when Annette became too ill to travel any further,' she told him. 'Mme Bézier knew of an inn where they would be safe, it is called Le Coq d'Or. My cousin and Annette stayed there and Annette's mother and her brother Edouard were taken straight to England. We waited for news from Neufchâtel, but none came, so my father got in touch with Mme Bézier and we arrived in St Pierre yesterday. We travelled in this wagon to Neufchâtel, only to find Annette in hysterics and my cousin in the lock-up. You know the rest, for Mme Bézier went straight for my father.' She paused and looked at him, catching his expression in deep thought. 'Did you hear me, Harvey?' she asked him.

'Yes, yes, of course I did. I am just working out the best way of going about things. Do you think that I would be able to hire a carriage in Dieppe?'

She looked surprised. 'You need a carriage?'

He nodded with impatience. 'Yes, of course I do. I am travelling as an English gentleman and Desmond will drive me. He is a man of many parts, I could not do without him.'

'Dieppe is quite a busy port. I am sure that you could procure a carriage there. Then it is not far to Neufchâtel. All I can say is good luck.'

'There is one other thing, Marianne, and this concerns you and Annette and Luke.'

'We are to wait here for you?'

'Yes, you are to wait here, but not for me,' he told her.

'What do you mean?' she asked him.

'If I succeed in releasing the count, I want to get him to London as quickly as possible. It is safer and much quicker to travel from Calais to Dover and I have arranged for the *Marie Rose* to wait at Calais for us. There are so may sailing vessels at Calais that she will not be noticed; at St Pierre she is too conspicuous. So from Neufchâtel, Desmond will drive along the coast road and all being well, we will reach Calais tonight and be at Dover early tomorrow morning. We will see to our business in London and the count will travel into Sussex in the evening.'

'You have timed it very closely, Harvey.'

'Yes, it is deliberate. I must trust to fate.'

'And what about us?' Marianne asked.

'You will stay here until I send the *Marie Rose* for you.'

'You will come for us?'

Harvey shook his head. 'No, I will stay in London. I will send a message to your father to get in touch with the Béziers and they will come for you. You must be prepared to wait for two or three days . . . you are frowning again. What is it this time?'

'It is Annette,' Marianne said slowly. 'She is so concerned for her father. How will she know that he is safe?'

'It is easy: I will try and send a message, but if that is impossible and I don't return this evening, she will know that her father is on his way to London. Do you think that will satisfy her, Marianne?'

'Yes, I think so. She will have confidence in you.'

'And you, do you have confidence in me?' Harvey asked softly. 'We did quarrel.'

'I must forget it,' she answered, then added to herself 'and the kiss'.

'I did not treat you very well, Marianne. Shall I make amends?' She could not guess his meaning until he took her hands. 'I will kiss you as a brother would.'

She ignored his words. 'I have to thank you for coming, Harvey.'

'Then you can kiss *me*.'

Without thinking, she reached up and kissed his cheek.

'Thank you, Marianne, that was very nice. Now let us go and fetch Desmond and we will be on our way. And I want to ask Annette if she has a ring or a brooch, something that will identify me to her father in case he does not remember me.'

★　★　★

The pair of them set off and it could be seen that Mr Harvey Burrage-Smith, Member of Parliament, was a very superior gentleman, used to giving orders and having them obeyed on the instant.

Their first obstacle was at the entrance to Dieppe where the guard immediately recognized the wagon.

'Monsieur,' said the guard, looking first at Desmond who sat up stiff and silent. 'This wagon belongs to the family of M. Franchot. It has been backwards and forwards several times to fetch the family to the party for the young man and his pretty sweetheart.'

Harvey nodded briefly and spoke in fluent French. 'Yes, you are right. M. Franchot has let us have the loan of it. I am required urgently in Paris and need to hire a carriage — with two horses, if possible. It will be more speedy. Please tell me whom I can approach for the hire of a carriage.'

'Yes, yes, of course. You need to go along to the harbour, it is no distance. Jacques Bouger and his brother, they will have a respectable and swift carriage for a gentleman such as yourself. Along this road and keep to the left, you will be there in minutes and . . . '

But his words were lost as the wagon disappeared along the road.

The guard was left scratching his head. This begins to look suspicious, he told himself, perhaps I should have questioned him further. I will do so on his return. Meanwhile, Harvey was making an arrangement with the Bouger brothers who were more than willing to make such a lucrative deal, even though there were certain conditions attached to it.

Harvey was precise in his instructions. 'We go to Neufchâtel and then to Calais in order to cross to Dover. If you will tell me the name of a good inn at Calais, your carriage and horses will be left there and everything paid for. You can collect them tomorrow morning unless you hear from me again.'

In minutes, Desmond was driving out of Dieppe in a trim carriage pulled by a pair of handsome bays. Harvey sat quietly, not bothering to look out of the window, but concentrating his thoughts on the difficult matter ahead.

They pulled up in the yard of Le Coq d'Or and the landlord came rushing out to see who his stylish visitors were. When Harvey asked for the town prison, the landlord knew instantly that it was good news, but gave no sign of his feelings.

'Along this road and to the right of the town square. You will find it easily,' he said.

Harvey thanked him and told Desmond to stay with the carriage, not to unharness the horses, but to be ready to be off at a moment's notice.

Desmond knew his master well, but could not stop his objection. 'Mr Harvey, you may need help. Would it not be better if I came with you . . . ?'

He was cut short. 'If I need help, I will come back for you. The important thing, Desmond, is to get away quickly.'

'Yes, sir,' answered Desmond, meekly enough.

Harvey sauntered through the town — it was the only way to describe his leisurely pace. He found the prison easily; a squat, brick building with only two small windows, up and down. He did not knock, but walked straight in, finding himself in a small office where two men were sitting and drinking coffee. One was in the uniform of a guard, the other a soldier, but of no rank. They did not even rise from their chairs when Harvey entered, but looked at him with lazy surprise.

Harvey knew that his first question would be his most difficult for he had no idea what the count was calling himself.

'Monsieur?' said one of the men at last.

'Good morning, I have come to Neufchâtel to see a gentleman who is staying at Le Coq d'Or, but the landlord tells me that he was brought to the prison yesterday.'

'M. Maurice? Yes, he is here. What do you want with him? You are very smart and from your dress and your accent, I believe you must be from England . . . though I do admit to you speaking in excellent French. I repeat, what do you want with M. Maurice? He pretends to be a farm worker, but he was heard to speak as a gentleman; we bring him here and await our instructions from Paris.

He may be wanted by Madame la Guillotine for all we know.'

'May I see him?'

The two men looked at each other; then the soldier nodded and the guard reached for a large key which hung from a hook above the table.

There appeared to be two cells, two identical doors, side by side. From inside one of them could be heard the sound of someone singing in a loud, hoarse voice.

The guard grinned. 'Mme Chenille, she has been at the cognac again. I think she does it to get a good place to sleep and something to eat for her breakfast. No matter. Here is M. Maurice.'

The door was opened wide and Harvey saw a tall man in a farm smock sitting silently on a bench. For a second, the captive's eyes registered surprise when he saw his visitor and he rose from his seat. Harvey put out a hand to shake hands in the English fashion and the count — for it was him — accepted. They had met once before in England and Harvey knew that he had been recognized. Their hands clasped, and in the grip, Harvey succeeded in pressing into the count's palm Annette's small enamel brooch in the shape of a diamond and with a raised rose at its centre.

Harvey could see from the count's grip on the brooch — his knuckles showed white — that the man in front of him knew that it had come from Annette; the look which passed between them said 'trust me and do whatever I say'.

The soldier clicked handcuffs on to the prisoner's wrists and he was taken into the office. The four of them sat facing each other.

'What do you want with M. Maurice?' asked the guard.

Harvey spoke boldly. 'I will tell you what you have already guessed; M. Maurice is no farm worker. He is the Comte d'Amand from Auteuil near Paris.'

'So I am right to take him back to Paris if I have the orders?' asked the soldier. 'And would you mind telling us exactly who you are who comes seeking him. And from England, too.'

Be careful, very careful, said Harvey to himself. All the time the count was watching him very closely.

'I will explain,' Harvey started slowly, 'that in England, there are a lot of people who admire the principles of the Revolution in France. We, too, have suffered from bad monarchs and look for a better rule. I am a Member of Parliament and my name is Mr

Harvey Burrage-Smith; I have Whig tendencies which you would not understand. The important thing is this: we have in England the Society for Constitutional Reform and we look to what is going on in France with interest. The Comte d'Amand, whom you are holding here, has an English wife and she is in England now, along with their children. We at the Society think that the count could be of great assistance to us in our own revolution and I have come with orders to try and get him released.'

'And how, monsieur, did you know that he was in captivity?'

'It is quite simple. You will know that his daughter was at the inn when he was taken — was it you that brought him here?' Harvey asked the soldier.

'Yes, it was me, and I left his daughter locked in. You mean that she has been taken to England?'

Harvey nodded, and glancing up saw a shadow of a smile passing over the count's face. 'Yes, she is safe and it has been easy for me to follow her directions to the inn. You must understand that I want to take him back to England with me; he will be of more use to our own revolution than to die at the hands of yours.' He paused and looked from one to the other. The count motionless, the guard frowning and there was no doubt about the look of greed in the soldier's face. Harvey could guess what was coming next and was prepared.

'Mon ami,' said the soldier to the guard, as though in confidence, 'I think that I could let monsieur go for some little consideration. I need not go back to Paris, but to my people in Dijon; M. Robespierre and his minions would not look for me there.'

'And you?' Harvey addressed the guard.

'For the same consideration,' replied the guard, 'I would say that M. Maurice had escaped and Barbot, here, has gone after him.'

Harvey stood up. 'It is done and I thank you for your cooperation.' He put his hand into the large pocket of his coat and drew out two wads of notes which he handed to each of the men.

When they saw the thickness and value of the notes, a smile spread over their faces and they hastily stuffed the notes into their own pockets.

'Thank you, monsieur,' said the soldier. 'I will unlock the handcuffs and get the bag of M. Maurice from the cell.'

Harvey felt stiff with the effort he had made, but inwardly, he rejoiced. The worst part was over.

He took up the canvas bag and offered his arm to the count 'Come along then, M. Maurice,' he said, and the oddly assorted pair walked free from the town jail.

# 6

Mr Harvey Burrage-Smith and Le Comte d'Amand hurried through the square at Neufchâtel and back to the inn; the square was busy with people and they attracted no attention. They said nothing to each other.

In the courtyard of the inn, they found a boy at the horses' heads and the landlord talking to Desmond. As the two gentlemen approached, the landlord smiled broadly.

'You are free, monsieur, it gives me great pleasure.'

The count frowned. 'But my Annette, where is she?'

The landlord put out a hand. 'Mademoiselle has been rescued and she is safe. The English gentleman will tell you.'

Harvey nodded. 'Yes, all is well, but we must hurry.' He turned to the landlord. 'Tell me, does your boy ride? Have you a fast mount?'

'Yes, of course.'

Harvey went up to the lad who had heard what had been said and was interested.

'Listen, you are to ride to St Pierre-sur-Mer — avoid Dieppe if you can — and when you reach the village, you must ask for the cottage of Mme Franchot. When you find her, you are to say only three words: 'all is well'. You will remember the message?'

'Mme Franchot, all is well — but yes, monsieur. Thank you.' The last as he pocketed the coin which Harvey held out to him.

Before Harvey could thank the landlord, the count spoke for the first time. 'Mr Burrage-Smith — I have that right? — I cannot go to London tomorrow in a farmer's smock. What shall I do?'

Harvey gave a laugh. 'I thought of it and my valet has a bag with some clothes of your cousin, Sir Thomas Welford, who said that he was the same build as you. Run into the inn quickly and change.'

'Your old room is empty, monsieur,' said the landlord.

It was a different Comte d'Amand who returned to them. The jacket and breeches fitted well and were sober in colour; he had managed to brush his hair and Harvey nodded in approval.

'Good,' he said and turned once again to the landlord. 'We will bid you farewell and offer our thanks.'

Neither of the gentlemen spoke while Desmond made his way out of Neufchâtel

130

and found the Calais road. It was busy, but the road surface was adequate and they made good speed, passing heavier farm wagons with ease.

Harvey remained silent, he knew that the count would want to speak in his own good time. So far that morning, everything had gone according to plan — now there was only Calais to negotiate.

'Mr Burrage-Smith,' said the count at last, but Harvey objected.

'No, please call me Harvey. You will have remembered meeting me at Welford Grange. And I will call you Maurice, if you will permit.'

The count smiled. 'Certainly, I have no wish to be formal after all you have done for me. I expected to be on my way to the guillotine today.'

'It has been a pleasure, Maurice.'

'But there is so much I do not understand; and I am very worried about Annette. Do you know where she is? What was the strange message you sent with the boy? It gave nothing away.'

'I will simply tell you that we arranged for Annette to be taken to England, but she refused to go without you. She is lodged at St Pierre-sur-Mer; she will know from the message that you are safe and that she can

131

proceed to Sussex.'

Maurice de Charnay gave a deep sigh. 'I understand nothing, but I feel that I could cry with joy. Why have you done this for me? All that in the jail about the Revolution and how I could help you in England. What did it all mean?'

Harvey smiled. 'I had to invent a reason for your release and it worked, did it not?'

'But you have not involved me in politics in England? I do not wish for that.' The count sounded worried.

'No, it was no more than a pretext to get you out of France. But now we are safely on our way, we must behave very carefully.'

'Tell me what I must do.'

'Do you speak English?' asked Harvey.

The count nodded. 'Yes, I have learned from my dear wife. You know that she is English for you said so in the jail and, also, you have met her in Sussex. And if I might say so, sir, you speak excellent French, but with a patois, I seem to think.'

'I will tell you about it one day,' Harvey replied.

'Who are you then, if I might ask?'

'I am a Member of Parliament and I sit on the Whig benches; and, as you know, I am a very near neighbour of your cousin, Sir Thomas Welford. I know him very well.'

'Ah, I begin to understand. My wife and Edouard reached Welford Grange safely? It was heartbreaking to see them go, but I had every confidence in the two Béziers. Madame Bézier, in particular, seemed to have her wits about her.' He paused as though working things out in his mind. 'But why was it that Edouard did not return for us?'

'It was not considered safe to have the two of you in France at the same time. Sir Thomas's son and daughter came over to fetch Annette. Marianne and Luke are with her now in St Pierre.'

At last, the face of the count showed a broad smile. 'It begins to make sense. They are good children though I suppose I must call them children no longer. I seem to remember on our last visit to Welford Grange that Annette who was very young and small for her age, was taken with Luke. He completely ignored her!'

Harvey grinned. 'I think now that we might have the beginnings of a romance on our hands!'

'It is good. I long to see them again. I cannot believe that we are on our way.'

'There are still some bridges to cross, we must take care.'

The scene in Calais was chaotic. Carriages and wagons choked the narrow streets, but

Harvey, asking directions only once, located the inn which the Bouger brothers had mentioned to him. It was easy to make the arrangements for the carriage and horses to be left there and after sitting in a corner of a noisy taproom for a simple meal and some wine, Harvey and his companion walked together in the direction of the harbour.

Traffic between England and France was frequent in spite of the trouble in France. Smuggling was at its peak, for the heavy taxes on wines and brandy in England had resulted in a busy and very lucrative trade in getting these commodities illicitly across the channel.

The harbour was choked with boats of all descriptions, but it was not difficult for Harvey to pick out the *Marie Rose*, nor to find a lad with a rowing boat to take them to the yacht.

They reached Dover with no delay and by the following morning, they were on their way to London, where later in the day, Harvey put the count on the coach which would take him into Sussex.

★   ★   ★

While this venture had been successfully accomplished, the three young people in St Pierre-sur-Mer were restless.

The boy from Le Coq d'Or arrived and gave Mme Franchot the brief message. Annette threw herself into Luke's arms and wept; he had become quite protective towards her.

'Luke, I now know that all is well. I am crying with joy and I promise that I will shed no more tears.'

'I do understand, Annette,' he replied gently. 'It has been a terrible time for you and your illness will have made you weak. I will ask Mme Franchot if there is a walk we can take tomorrow morning; along the sands would not be safe for we would easily be seen.'

Marianne was watching them with amusement; suddenly, her little brother seemed to have grown into a caring young gentleman, and it was not difficult to see how Annette regarded Luke. If they find a walk, she said to herself, I will make an excuse and not accompany them. They need to get to know each other a little better, and in happier circumstances.

Mme Franchot was applied to the next day and agreed that the sands were not safe. St Pierre-sur-Mer was a natural inlet along the coast between Dieppe and Fécamp and there were cliffs on each side of the small sandy bay.

'Monsieur Luke,' the Frenchwoman said readily. 'I would advise you to walk along the lane at the back of the cottage; this will bring you to the West Cliff. It is steep, but worth the climb, you will find.'

When it seemed evident that Marianne was not preparing to set off with them, Annette questioned her. 'Marianne, you are not ready. Where is your shawl?'

Marianne smiled. 'I will not come if you don't mind. I think it would be wise for one of us to be here in case of any message arriving. 'We are not out of the wood yet' as the saying goes.'

Annette's face fell. 'Do you think we should not go? Is it proper for me to go with Luke when there are only the two of us?'

Marianne's smile turned to a laugh. 'You are cousins, Annette, and I think that a walk and some fresh sea air will do you a lot of good.'

Annette gave her a kiss. 'You are good, Marianne. I am sorry that it is not right between you and Mr Harvey. He is a fine gentleman and I shall never be able to thank him enough for going to free papa.'

'Harvey and I had a quarrel and that is the end of it.'

Luke appeared and he and Annette set off to find the cliff path. October had departed in high winds and November had come in brisk and cold; but that morning, the sun appeared fitfully from high white clouds. Annette felt easy for the first time for many days.

'Luke, it is good of you to bring me for a walk. You would not have done that two years ago when I was only thirteen; you took no notice of me!'

He laughed. 'I remember you as just a plain little girl not even out of the schoolroom; don't forget that I was seventeen and considered myself the young gentleman.' He looked down at her; she is still plain, I suppose, he thought, but there is something about her. Perhaps it is her courage and she has the lovely blue eyes of the Vilvens, just like Lucy. He said as much. 'You are grown up now, Annette, and I notice your blue eyes, for they are like your mothers and my mother's, too. Lucy has the blue eyes, as well; I wonder how she is getting on with Edouard?'

'You think there is a romance there, Luke?'

'I would not be surprised; they seem to be very taken with one another.' He paused and looked about him. 'The path is getting steep, Annette, we had better save our breath for our climb. Give me your hand.'

Annette hardly needed the invitation, and they took the steep, rough path up the cliff.

They stopped at the top and Annette sighed as she looked around her. 'It is so beautiful, the sea sparkles and St Pierre looks so small. My poor country, how can there be so much beauty here when in Paris, all is violence and hatred and blood.'

Luke was looking down at her with concern, she had been through so much. 'It will be hard for you to forget, little one. Perhaps you will have to marry me and make your home in England.' He saw a flush come into her face and regretted his remark.

'You must not say such things, Cousin Luke, it is not right to jest about something so serious.'

He bent down and kissed her on the forehead. 'There, that is to say I am sorry. We are both young. Am I forgiven?'

She smiled then. 'Of course I can forgive you when you kiss me so nicely . . . ' She broke off and pointed out to sea. 'Luke, there is a yacht. Do you suppose it is the *Marie Rose* come for us?'

He looked carefully. 'I don't think that I would recognize her at this distance, but she is sailing away from St Pierre and coming in this direction. I am afraid that we may have many days to wait yet and we do not know who will come for us.'

As it happened, the next days turned cold

and stormy, with dark clouds and sudden squalls of heavy rain. They were confined to the cottage, but Mme Franchot saved the day by producing a pack of cards. There was a lot of fun and laughter while Luke and Marianne tried to teach Annette how to play commerce.

On the third day, they all felt sure that the *Marie Rose* would come and stayed glued to the window all the morning. They were not to be disappointed. Luke and Annette spotted the white sails at the same time, and Marianne, who had been practising her French with Mme Franchot in the kitchen, ran into the living-room to join them.

When they saw two figures step out of the waiting rowing boat, they were in no doubt that it was the Béziers who had come for them.

And from what they could see under the now familiar black bonnet, it was a smiling Mme Bézier who entered the cottage.

'How are you, my children?' she said jovially. 'I hope you are ready to return to England.'

Annette could hardly bear to ask the question. 'Papa . . . is he all right?'

'Yes, little one, he is safely at Welford Grange with your mama and Edouard, and they all wait for your return.'

Marianne could not stop herself from

asking about Harvey. 'And Mr Burrage-Smith, madame, is he there, too? You did not come that time, did you? He was very rude and said he would not have you with him because you talked too much!'

Mme Bézier gave her usual cackle. 'He is particular, that one. He wanted to go for the count on his own. Maybe he was right for it was difficult and Bézier and myself were becoming too well known.'

'Do you know if he is in Sussex?'

'I am not sure, mademoiselle, I think it was his intention to stay in London. Now, are you all packed up and ready to go? We must thank Mme Franchot and be on our way. I will warn you that the crossing will be a little rough today, but we must hope to reach Newhaven before dark. Sir Thomas will be waiting for us.'

The crossing *was* rough, but the three young people enjoyed it and none of them was afflicted with sea-sickness.

At Newhaven, Sir Thomas was on his own with the carriage, and soon had them back at Welford Grange.

They had all said goodbye rather sadly to M. and Mme Bézier and told them that they would never be forgotten. Mme Bézier was anxious to be on her way and cheerfully told them that if they did meet again, neither of them would be recognized. Their work went on, but they did not wear the same clothes all the time.

At Welford Grange, it was a noisy meeting with tears and laughter and joy. Annette clung to her mother and father and introduced Luke particularly, as if they had not known him since he was a child.

The de Charnays stayed for a week at Welford Grange; Luke returned to Oxford after a fond farewell to Annette. Edouard and Lucy were to be seen everywhere together and Marianne was wondering if there would be an announcement.

For herself, Marianne found that she was thinking of Harvey and the strange circumstance of him being the person who had travelled to France to obtain the release of the count from jail, then bringing him safely back to England and his family. She was grateful to him, but had not had the opportunity of thanking him. It seemed that his duties in Westminster were keeping him in London.

As the days went by, she forgot about Harvey in her concern for Lucy.

Her sister became very quiet after the de Charnay family had left them, and Marianne considered that Lucy was making herself weak and ill. That part of the cause of this lassitude was the absence of Edouard was evident, but Marianne had an instinctive feeling that Lucy was worrying herself into a decline over something more serious.

The cold and wet November weather did not help as they were not able to ride and had to be content with their embroidery, their books and their music.

One morning, when clear skies and pale sunshine brought their first hard frost, Marianne persuaded Lucy to put on her warmest dress and cape and to walk over to the Burberry's farm with her. Mrs Burberry had not been well and Sir Thomas had asked Marianne to go and see her and to take some of his home-brewed ale; he thought it would 'build her up' as he put it.

Walking along and looking at Lucy's pale face, Marianne was thinking that it was Lucy who would benefit from their father's ale. I will be careful how I ask her about Edouard, she said to herself, for I am sure that he is the cause of Lucy's unhappines.

'Have you had a letter from Edouard?' she asked quietly as they made their way across the hard ground, white with frost.

Lucy sounded cross. 'You know I have not, I would have told you.'

Marianne was pleased with the terseness of the reply and pressed her point so that Lucy would have to answer her. 'Did he say that he

142

would write to you?'

'No, he did not, but I did hope to hear from him.'

'Did you quarrel, Lucy? I cannot help but notice that you seem out of sorts.'

Lucy turned to look at her sister. I do not wish to talk about it,' she said shortly.

'Oh come, Lucy, we have always told each other everything. You seemed so happy when I returned from France, but since our cousins removed to London, it seems to me that you are very downcast. I can only think that it is something to do with Edouard.'

It seemed as though the name itself touched Lucy where Marianne's questions had failed. They had reached the stile into the next field, and the basket containing the ale was handed across while each girl climbed over. It seemed natural to pause there for Lucy put her arms around Marianne and hugged her.

'You are a dear sister. Yes, it is to do with Edouard. We do love each other and I accept that he cannot think of marriage until he has found some position in this country. Before he went to London, I thought he would say something about it and that he would speak to father, but he just told me he loved me and not to forget him, and that was all. And I love him so much and it is so hard and . . . oh, Marianne.'

'Now, no tears,' said Marianne as they set off towards the farm. 'Edouard is the vicomte and a gentleman of honour and as soon as he knows what he is to do in this country, I am sure that he will say the right thing to you, Lucy. Please do not make yourself ill over it.'

Lucy sighed, but without her former hopelessness. 'You are very good to me, but I am sure you can never have loved as I love Edouard, even though you were betrothed to Harvey.'

Marianne, who was in two minds about her feelings for Harvey and who found it hard to forget the unexpected passion of his kiss, was pleased to hear the brightening of Lucy's tone.

'Edouard will do his best for you and as soon as he has settled his affairs, he will come rushing down here at breakneck speed with a ring in his pocket.'

This produced the laugh from Lucy which Marianne had hoped for.

'I promise to be more patient, Marianne, and thank you. Look, here we are at the farm already. Now we must try and cheer up poor Mrs Burberry.'

★ ★ ★

But their next visitor was not to be the Vicomte d'Amand, but Mr Harvey Burrage-Smith. He had not been seen for some time and Marianne had imagined him to be still in London.

The cold snap over, Marianne and Lucy had taken to riding out again and one morning as they were crossing the park towards the village, they were surprised to see someone galloping towards them.

Marianne recognized Harvey and they stopped so that they could speak to him.

His riding-coat was a brown that was almost black, his stock cream and he looked very handsome. Lucy glanced at her sister and was not surprised to see the expression of surprised pleasure on Marianne's face.

'Good morning, young ladies,' was Harvey's greeting and Marianne thought she could detect a hint of levity.

'I was riding over to Welford Grange in search of you, Marianne.'

'I thought you to be still in London, sir,' Marianne said, trying to hide her sense of happiness at seeing him again.

'Parliament has risen, thank God. Sometimes I wonder why I ever went into politics. And now we have all the trouble of the Duke of York commanding a pathetic force against

145

the French in the Netherlands. Pitt is no man of war, and Grenville not much better.'

'You think the Revolution is over then?' she asked him.

He shook his head. 'Not as long as Robespierre lives. No one is safe, even though they do their best to raise their own army in France, which is more than can be said of Pitt here in England.'

Marianne looked at him suspiciously. 'Have you changed your views, Harvey? Not so long ago, you would have been rushing over to Robespierre's side.'

He was not abashed and gave a grin. They had ridden back with him and had reached Welford Grange. 'Leave your horse, Marianne, and walk in the wood with me. Goodbye, Lucy, it has given me great pleasure to see you again.'

Marianne waited while Harvey took the horses to the stables; she felt pleased to be with him again and hoped that there was not going to be another argument about the political situation in France.

She liked walking in the wood; it was, in fact, no more than a copse and bordered Sir Thomas's land where it met the estate of Lord Kentish towards Lewes. It had been planted over fifty years earlier to afford shelter to the memorial to the Sir Thomas

Welford who was Marianne's great-great-grandfather. The memorial was an oblong solid stone with Sir Thomas's name and dates carved on the sides; on the two ends, were carvings of his favourite dogs and as a child, Marianne had loved it. Later, she was told that Sir Thomas had designed it himself and she admired him for it.

That day, Marianne walked silently at Harvey's side and the silence was not broken until they reached the memorial and stood against it.

'You are very quiet today, Harvey.'

'Yes, I was trying to pluck up courage to talk to you about our marriage.'

She looked at him in astonishment, could he be serious?

'But we quarrelled,' she said.

'Yes, I know, I was sorry afterwards.'

No words of love, Marianne told herself before she replied. 'But it was a fundamental disagreement. I could not marry anyone who was in favour of the Revolution and sided with the butchers and the murderers of France.'

'*I think I might have misled you about that, mademoiselle,*' Harvey said to her and he spoke in French patois.

Marianne stood rigid with shock.

She looked around and saw that they were

alone. She looked up at Harvey; his dark eyes were regarding her steadily, his mouth straight and serious.

'Would you mind saying that again,' she whispered hoarsely.

'Certainly, Mademoiselle Marianne, I think I might have misled you.'

Mme Bézier.

It was the voice of Mme Bézier coming from Harvey's lips.

Marianne stammered. 'You . . . you are very good at imitations, Harvey. I did not know that you had ever met Mme Bézier and certainly not to imitate her patois so accurately.'

'Look at me, Marianne,' Harvey said in his own voice.

Marianne did look at him, and she saw the Harvey she had known all her life.

'You are Harvey Burrage-Smith.'

'I am Mme Bézier, Marianne.'

Again he used the peculiar accent and the cracked high-pitched voice so unlike his own deep tones.

Marianne went wild.

She took him by the arm, then thumped her fists against his chest. He did not move or say another word.

'You cannot be Mme Bézier. How is it possible? You are the Harvey I have always known. I would have recognized you. You are teasing me. Making fun of me. Mme Bézier was an old French countrywoman, she came from the south, I am sure of it. That was why her patois seemed strange to us. Our French was learned in the schoolroom; and I would know you anywhere, Harvey. Why are you tormenting me like this?'

She found herself pulled gently against him, she was without a hat and he stroked her hair.

'Never mind, Marianne,' he said softly. 'Do you ever remember seeing Mme Bézier's face?'

Marianne drew back and looked hard at his familiar face. Was there anything about it which suggested Mme Bézier?

'The bonnet, Marianne?' he murmured.

She remembered the big, black bonnet which was so old, it flopped over her face; she remembered, too, that she had wondered how the old lady could possibly have seen where she was driving.

'That bonnet, it hid your face, however did you see . . . oh, was it really you, Harvey? I cannot believe it. You will have a lot of explaining to do . . . how *did* you see, as a matter of interest?'

'I could see very little, I had to rely on Desmond.'

'Desmond?' Not another shock, Marianne thought. 'You mean . . . you mean — '

'My husband was also my valet. I never could do without him so he became M. Bézier. The trouble was that he spoke very little French, though he understood it quite well.'

Marianne was still staring at him, and she was beginning to believe him. 'That was why I thought I had seen him before, yet he was different. How was that, Harvey?'

'It was the clothes and the beret and a little charcoal, my dear. We made his skin darker. It was surprising what a difference it made; I wore it, too, to make me look older.'

Marianne sighed and slumped against him; he held her close and she felt glad of his arms around her. 'I still cannot believe it, Harvey. Your voice, the patois, however did you manage a patois like that? It was perfect and you are English.'

'It was easy, my dear. You see, about ten years ago when I did the grand tour, I stayed with a family in a little village called Frontignac on the south coast of France. The nearest town was Sête and the nearest city was Montpellier. It is a beautiful old city with an ancient university. I liked it so much that my father agreed that I should read for my degree there instead of going to Oxford. I had four very happy years there and came away speaking French like a native. I could converse like a nobleman or chat in the local patois, which was a strange mixture of French and Spanish. Sête is near the Spanish border. That is why it was so easy to create Mme Bézier.'

'Yes, I see, I do see. But that is only the beginning,' said Marianne. 'Can we walk a little in the wood, Harvey? I am getting cold and there is so much I must ask you before we return.'

Still with his arms around her shoulders, they walked through the wood and Marianne learned all she wished to know. But her most immediate question was asked with great hesitation.

'Harvey, I do not understand why you have told me all this now. I need never have known the truth.'

He gave a short laugh. 'Do you not see, Marianne? I want only the truth between us for a special reason; I had to refuse you when you asked me to go for your cousins, because I was already committed to go as Mme Bézier. That was when we quarrelled.'

'But, Harvey,' she worried at him. 'We quarrelled about your politics, about your views of the Revolution. I could not marry a gentleman so entirely in favour of all the dreadful things which were going on in France.'

'Marianne,' he said gently. 'I will tell you in the greatest confidence because I know I can trust you. I have led a life of lies for many years. I have professed my views to be pro-Revolution in parliamentary circles, so that I would be the last person to be suspected of going into France to bring the noble émigrés over to England. Do you understand that?'

'Do you mean that the de Charnays were not the first family you had brought to England?'

'No, they were one of many.'

'And did you always go as Mme Bézier?' she asked.

He shook his head and smiled at her. 'No, it is not possible to use the same disguise too many times. I have been as a *curé*, a wine merchant, Desmond and I even went once as father and son.'

'But you went back for the count as yourself. Why was that? However did you manage it?'

'With much haste and a great urgency; I was afraid that he would be taken to Paris,' he replied. 'I had to return to England as Mme Bézier, change my clothes very quickly and set off again. You see, Marianne, it was different that time. The count was in jail and I had to use my skills as a sympathizer of the Revolution to free him. I pretended that he would be useful to us in England; the ruse worked fortunately. I have to admit that his guards were very easily taken in, especially when I produced a roll of bank notes.'

'We will never be able to thank you properly. But even that was not the end of it. The count told us that you had stayed in London, when all the time, you must have been chasing down to Sussex to become Mme Bézier again so that you could come and fetch us. When we said goodbye to you, it really was goodbye, wasn't it? Does it mean an end to your capers abroad? Do you stay in England now, Harvey?'

'I go to London tomorrow to receive my orders. I think that with the war in the Netherlands and France now our enemy, there may not be another time. I wanted to see you to explain everything before I went off to London; I did not like to quarrel with you. Perhaps one day, when it is all over, I will be able to ask you once again to marry me. Do you think you will be able to say yes, Marianne? No, do not reply, I will find the answer in my own way.'

He turned and pulled her roughly towards him and her cloak fell to the ground.

'No, Harvey,' she protested.

'Yes, Marianne.'

She could feel the steely strength of him against her as he kissed her, slowly asking for a response from her lips — and finding it.

'Thank you, Marianne,' he murmured as he picked up her cloak and wrapped it round her. 'I think you have told me and I will be back to demand an answer very soon.'

And completely turning the subject, he said they would walk back to Welford Grange; there, he retrieved his horse and rode off with a cheery goodbye and with no words of love.

Marianne sighed and watched him go.

# 7

For a whole day, Marianne thought about Harvey and the revelations he had made to her; she walked alone and said nothing about him to her family, except to tell Lucy that he had returned to London.

She was still in a state of disbelief that Harvey and Mme Bézier could possibly have been one and the same person; but that had not been the only shock. She had disagreed with Harvey's attitudes and beliefs towards the Revolution for so long, that she now found it hard to come to terms with the fact that his political stance had been a lie. That in all these last years, he had behaved with courage and daring in bringing the émigrés to England; that these actions of his had secured the safety of her own cousins.

When he arrived at Welford Grange, just as they were finishing dinner the next day, she assumed that he had not gone to London as he had planned.

It soon became obvious that his visit was an urgent one.

Marianne, Lucy and Lady Welford had just returned from the dining-room to the drawing-room when Harvey was announced; Sir Thomas was enjoying his glass of port in the library.

Harvey glanced round the room and said a brief good evening to Lady Welford and Lucy; then he went up to Marianne.

'I thought you to be in London,' she said as she withdrew her hand from his.

'I have been in London and I have journeyed straight back. I have to see your father, Marianne, and I will speak to you afterwards.'

He hurried from the room and Marianne thought him not as immaculate as usual; his topcoat was slung over his shoulders and his cravat — for Harvey — was very loosely arranged.

Ten minutes later, her father called her to the library.

She hurried in with great curiosity to find her father looking very serious and standing by the fireplace talking to Harvey.

'My dear Marianne,' Sir Thomas said as he came up to her. 'Harvey has come on a most urgent matter and it concerns you very closely. I am going to leave you to talk it over with him. I have given my permission as I believe you to be a sensible and resourceful young lady; it might be in your power to do something very courageous. Harvey, I shall be in the drawing-room if you should need me.'

He left them and Marianne turned to Harvey; his eyes were searching her face and he held out a hand and led her to one of the fireside chairs; for himself, he pulled up a straight-backed chair from the desk and sat beside her.

'Marianne, you must be wondering what all this is about. I had better tell you what has happened on this rather eventful day. I did go to London as I had told you was my intention. I left Broadoaks in the carriage with Desmond at first light and we made good time; at least the roads were dry. At the House, I was asked to go and see Lord Grenville — he is Foreign Secretary, as you know. He thanked me for bringing the de Charnays over safely and told me that he had hoped that it would be my last mission; we were on the brink of a full-scale war with France, he said very soberly. But something very urgent and rather pitiful had come about and he considered that I was the only person he could ask to resolve the matter.' He stopped speaking and put his hand on her shoulder. 'I am sorry, this is going to take a long time in the telling, you will have to be patient with me.'

Marianne nodded, but said nothing; what intrigued her was how anything connected with Harvey's activities could involve her. Unless it is something to do with my cousins, she said to herself.

Harvey continued, speaking rather quickly. 'The situation is this. The Foreign Office has received an urgent request from Forster's Banking Company in the City. One of their staff, who has been living in Paris with his wife for two years, has gone to the guillotine. His name is Mr Charles Bolton and it seems that his poor young wife — now a widow, of course — is being held in captivity; but she has managed to send the company a message. As you can imagine, it has taken a long time in the coming and it is imperative that we take action immediately . . . what is it?' he asked as he saw her frown.

'Harvey, how can this possibly affect me? I am very sorry for the young lady, but I do not see how I can help.'

He took her hands and she could feel the strength and stress in his. 'I am coming to it. I am to go over to Paris first thing tomorrow morning; I will go by Newhaven to save having to travel back to London and then on to Dover. But, Marianne, we have decided that a young lady must accompany me; Esther Bolton — the young woman in Paris — will be in desperate need of female company. It is not sufficient — or proper

— for me to go to fetch her on my own. We do have a gentleman who works with his wife on these missions, but they are already in France. Lord Grenville asked me to find a strong-minded young lady to go with me. I immediately thought of you.'

Marianne stared at him. 'You think of me as strong-minded?'

He gave a smile. 'Remember our quarrel? Then how you did not hesitate to go with Luke to fetch Annette.'

She still stared. 'But I don't understand. Yes, I am willing to go, but how can we travel to Paris together? You are a gentleman and I am a lady, Harvey.' As she spoke she gave a sudden chuckle. 'I expect you have worked it all out.'

'You are willing to do it?' he asked her.

'Yes, I will do it, Harvey, or I will do my best especially if my father has given his permission. He is a good man and always acts for the best.'

'Thank you, my dear,' he said and leaned forward and kissed her on the cheek.

She blushed with the pleasure of his lips on her skin, but spoke briskly to hide it. 'Now tell me.'

'What I propose is this; I have thought of several alternatives and I think that I have found the most satisfactory one. You and I will travel as man and wife . . . what is it, for the love of God?'

Marianne was scandalized. 'But we will be away at least two nights — how can we possibly stay at an inn as man and wife? It is not possible, you know very well that I would never agree to it. And what was Papa thinking of?'

He was getting angry. 'Will you stop interrupting. I assured you that I had thought of everything. There will be no need for us to stay at an inn. Over the years, we have found a string of what I would call 'safe' houses. Men and women and families who are against the outcome of the Revolution and keep their houses open for the English agents who travel backwards and forwards between the two countries . . . ' He paused, almost exasperated with her. 'What is it now?'

'I was only going to say like Mme Franchot in St Pierre-sur-Mer. You are very irritable today.'

'I have cause to be. I have been travelling non-stop, and getting in and out of London makes any journey very difficult. Farm wagons blocking the road, with curricles and phaetons trying to race between them, there is scarcely room for a carriage. I am fortunate in having Desmond, he is very patient.'

'I always thought of you as a patient person, Harvey.'

'Nonsense, you know only the country gentleman. One has the time to be patient in the countryside and Sussex is no exception. Now, once and for all, will you let me explain what we are to do?'

'Yes, Harvey,' returned Marianne with a pretence at meekness.

'We will travel as man and wife. I am not taking Desmond this time — he is most put out. But I want to pose as a coachman and I want you in the carriage as my wife. You speak French well, Marianne? I have only just thought of it; I suppose it is possible that the guards in Paris might question you.'

'You mean that we are travelling as a French couple?'

'Yes, of course; I think we will call ourselves Carnot. What about your command of the language?'

'We were all taught French by Biddy because of having French cousins. When they visited we talked in both French and English. And when we were in St Pierre the other day waiting to be brought home, I spent the time practising my French with Mme Franchot, especially when Luke and Annette went off for walks.'

'We have a romance there?' he asked and

161

his tone lightened for the first time.

'Yes, they are very young, but they seem to be quite taken with each other.'

'It is good to hear some pleasant news in all this turmoil. To continue, dear girl, you can find the clothes befitting the wife of a coachman? It will not do to be dressed as an elegant young lady.'

Marianne nodded. 'It will be no problem. Janey, my maid, is the same build as myself and I can borrow something from her. What about you?'

'I will be in livery. I had to obtain something in London before we left as Desmond is shorter than I am; he is thinner, too, so his clothes will not do for me.' He got up suddenly and paced about the room. 'I will tell you our exact arrangements. Early tomorrow morning, I will ride over for you and you are to be ready with only a small bag, if you please. Your father will take us to Newhaven where the *Marie Rose* will be waiting for us. I have already sent the order. We will cross to St Pierre and borrow the wagon once again; in Dieppe, I know where to go for a carriage. Then we travel to Paris. Are you prepared?'

'What about the guards at Paris?' she asked.

'You must follow my lead. I know where

Esther Bolton is being held; she is not in jail, but is held captive in the house of one of the guards. It will not be easy, Marianne, Paris is not a happy place.'

'I will have you with me and I will do whatever you tell me.'

He smiled for the first time. 'Like a good wife? Oh, it reminds me that I have a ring for you, it was my mother's. I hope it fits your finger. Hold out your hand.'

He came up to her and took a gold ring from his pocket. She held up her left hand to him and he slid the ring on to her third finger. It was loose.

'With this ring I thee wed, with my body I thee worship . . . ' he started to say, then their eyes met and they burst out laughing. It was as much laughter with the tension of the moment as of jollity.

Marianne finished for him: 'And with all my worldly goods I thee endow. Thank you, Harvey, that is very kind.'

He pulled her to her feet and into his arms. 'Minx,' he said. 'This is too serious an occasion for jesting, but we must be on good terms. No more quarrels and I think we will seal our married state with a kiss.'

'Harvey,' she objected, but she could say no more for his lips were on hers.

In the emotion of the moment, they clung

to each other and the tension was dissipated as warmth and passion passed between them.

Harvey lifted his head at last. 'I think you will make me a very suitable wife,' he told her lightly.

Marianne said nothing; had she spoken, she would have shown her tremendous pleasure at the embrace.

'You are silent, my dear, does it all worry you?'

'No, of course not,' she replied, speaking briskly to hide her feelings. 'What time do you wish me to be ready in the morning?'

'Be at the front of the Grange with your father at seven o'clock. It will be dark, but your coachman knows the way to Newhaven very well. And try and borrow a thick woollen mantle, we are well into November and it will be cold. Goodbye, I will see you in the morning.'

And he was gone, and Marianne stood looking after him. She had known Harvey all her life and thought she knew him well; now, in the space of a few weeks, it was as though she was getting to know someone she had met only recently.

At Newhaven the next morning, she was to find herself with an impatient Harvey. The *Marie Rose* was waiting for them and they were taken out in the rowing boat; and there on the yacht, they stayed. The sun was barely up and the day had started misty and still. There was not a breath of wind, but the master of the sailing boat was not despondent, telling Harvey that a fine and misty day often started very still, but as soon as the sun rose, a breeze would spring up. He thought that there would be enough wind to fill the sails within half an hour.

His prediction was right and in the time that they were waiting offshore, Harvey and Marianne went below and were given some breakfast. It was a simple meal of ham and fresh bread from the local baker; hot coffee was very welcome.

As the sun rose, the clouds came scudding past in a stiff breeze; they were under way in minutes and were soon speeding across the channel.

Marianne wrapped her thick woollen mantle around her and stood at the rail with Harvey; he was silent, but not unpleasantly so and she guessed his mind to be occupied with the difficulties lying ahead of them.

As he had said, he was dressed in the dark navy livery of a coachman; it had frogging of a lighter colour and gold buttons; it was also a very good fit and made him look distinguished rather than servile. This to

Marianne's amusement; she did not tell him her thoughts.

She, herself, was wearing one of Janey's warmer dresses under her mantle; it fitted well and Marianne felt snug, she had tied a small shawl around her head. The November wind off the cold sea did not chill her and she enjoyed watching the white spume of the wake of the yacht as she stood close to the silent Harvey.

All went well at St Pierre-sur-Mer, and they were soon on their way to Dieppe having been given a good meal by Mme Franchot. They did not know where their next meal would come from and Mme Franchot insisted on them putting buttered bread rolls and apples into their travelling bags.

The fiction started at the gate of Dieppe where the same guard thought that he recognized Harvey.

'Weren't you through in this wagon a few days ago?' he asked. 'You asked me where you could hire a carriage to take you to Calais. I sent you to the Bouger brothers down by the harbour.'

Harvey was shaking his head. 'No, you must be mistaken. One wagon looks like another.'

Marianne was sitting up next to Harvey and she saw the hesitation on the guard's face

166

when he heard that Harvey was speaking in his southern patois.

'Come to think of it,' said the guard, 'you was a proper gentleman and you had your servant with you — now you've got your missus. You got business in the town, then?'

'Yes, I have and I'd be grateful if you'd let me through quickly.'

'Certainly, sir.'

Harvey drove on to the harbour and both he and Marianne were laughing. 'He must be the most useless guard in France,' said Harvey, 'but it suits us, does it not, my dear wife?'

Marianne laughingly agreed.

A small carriage was procured, and with two horses; with Marianne safely installed inside and Harvey up front, they made haste along the busy road to Paris.

The guards at the North Gate into Paris were a different matter to the solitary guard at Dieppe and Marianne felt fearful. The tall wooden doors of the gate were closed and the scene outside them was both noisy and chaotic. Several carriages and wagons were pulled up, their owners standing at their horses' heads to try and stop them from rearing in fright at the crush, the noise and the spasmodic sound of gunfire.

Harvey got down from the carriage and

shouted inside to Marianne. 'I must see to the horses, you stay quiet and try and listen to what goes on. When it is our turn, they will probably question you, too.'

Marianne heard it all and could not help but admire Harvey in his audacity.

'Your pass?' the guard demanded.

Harvey handed over a square of paper and it was scrutinized.

'Jacques Carnot, that's a good name to have. You are related to the M. Carnot who is our great military leader?'

'No, he is no relation of mine. There are many with the name of Carnot.' Harvey's tone was brusque and cool at the same time.

'And your business?' was the next question.

'We go to my poor sister, Mme Francine Legros. Her husband has gone to the guillotine and only because he was chef to the Marquis de Vienne. I must go to her and take her safely to my home in Dieppe. My wife is in the carriage to take care of her.'

'You wife, too? It is not usual to bring one's womenfolk into the city. We will see.'

Marianne heard it all and trembled for a second. Have courage, she told herself, Harvey expects it of you.

The door opened and the guard spoke roughly, but did not touch her. 'Out you get, woman, let's learn what you have to say.'

Marianne got out of the carriage and Harvey was prevented from helping her.

'So who is this you take to your home, eh?'

'My poor sister-in-law, my Francine, her husband was taken from her.'

'And your name?'

'Mme Carnot.'

'And where do you come from?'

'From Dieppe,' Marianne replied and tried not to sound nervous.

Another guard was called and they spoke together for a long time. Marianne watched them anxiously, but tried not to show her anxiety in her expression. She could see Harvey out of the corner of her eye; he was standing impassively, one hand on the horses' reins, his whip in the other.

With shouting and banging and the neighing of frightened horses all round her, Marianne had an instinctive fear that all was not well.

From the office of the guards next to the gate, a senior officer was summoned; he was senior not only in his uniform, but in his bearing and his aggressive manner.

'What is it?' he said to the two guards who had summoned him.

'This man,' said the tallest of the guards, pointing to Harvey. 'He says he is from Dieppe and has come to take his widowed sister to his home. But, sir, you see, Léon here is from the south. His home is at Narbonne, it is nearly into Spain and he says that monsieur's patois is of that area; he recognizes it easily. It is nothing like that of Dieppe.'

Marianne had been able to follow all of this; she was still standing by the carriage and put out a hand to clutch at the door. She dared not look in Harvey's direction.

The officer walked up to Harvey.

'You are a coachman from Dieppe?'

'Yes, sir.' Harvey's tone was steady.

'Why do you speak the Narbonne patois?' he was asked.

'My family came from Sête, it is not far from Narbonne; we have lived in Dieppe for many years, but I have never lost the patois.'

'So, I understand — let me see your hands.'

Marianne held her breath, it was something they had not considered. She watched the taller guard take off Harvey's coachman's gloves and hold out his hands to the officer. She could see from where she was standing that Harvey's hands bore the pale mark of the gentleman.

'Aristo,' barked the officer. 'These are no coachman's hands. Now tell me who you are, if you please, or it will be straight to the Place de la Grève for you and your pretty wife.'

Marianne stood where she was, still clutching the carriage door; not one of them glanced at her, all eyes now on Harvey.

Then he turned and looked in her direction and their eyes met; she could read the message. *He would admit to them being English, better to be English than French aristocrats.*

'I am waiting for a reply.' The officer of the guard stood facing Harvey, his stance was threatening.

'I am Mr Harvey Burrage-Smith; I am a Member of Parliament in England.'

A scoffing laugh came from the officer. 'Mr Smith? That amuses me; are not all English gentlemen called Mr Smith when they are in trouble and trying to conceal their identity? Try again.'

Harvey's expression did not change, his voice was calm. 'You can call me Mr Burrage if you would prefer, it was my mother's name and it does not change the fact that I am a Member of Parliament. Mr Pitt would vouch for me, or Lord Grenville, the Foreign Secretary, who sent me here.'

'Very well, Mr Burrage-Smith, you are trying to be superior with me. That, I do not think I like. Now tell me the purpose of your visit and why you bring your wife to France with you. Perhaps you are just married and

171

thought you might try a visit to the continent for your honeymoon.'

He is trying to crack Harvey's coolness, thought Marianne, but he will not succeed.

'Monsieur,' said Harvey politely. 'My wife and I have come to Paris to find an English widow whose husband has gone to your guillotine. We used French names because we thought it would be safer, I deeply regret that my patois gave me away.'

'You speak excellent French, monsieur,' replied the officer. 'If it is of the south, it is of no consequence to me. I am more interested in the English widow you have come to save; are you sure it is not a family of aristocrats who try to escape to England?'

'I can tell you the young lady's name and I have her address.'

'Good, good, perhaps you would like to give it to me.'

'Would you prefer me to write it down? I believe that she is being kept in captivity.' Harvey was at his loftiest.

They are like cat and mouse, Marianne thought; can Harvey succeed? The French officer is very wily.

'No, just tell me the name, I have a good memory.'

'It is Mrs Esther Bolton and she is being held at number seven Rue de Brive.'

Marianne held her breath as the officer nodded. 'Interesting, very interesting. Wait here, monsieur, I will check my list of prisoners.' He walked back into the office and as Harvey moved towards Marianne, the guard closed in on him.

'Stay here,' said the one called Léon.

'I wish to have a word with my wife,' said Harvey firmly.

'Oh, very well then . . . miss, you come here.'

Marianne was escorted to where Harvey was still standing at the horses' heads. She felt his hand like steel on her arm and he whispered in English and very quickly. 'We are up against it, don't say anything unless you absolutely have to. And have courage . . . '

'Monsieur, you will please speak in French so that we can understand.'

'It is all right,' said Harvey, facing them boldly. 'I have just told her that I love her and that everything will be all right. Ah, here is your superior.'

The officer was back with them; he was holding a sheaf of papers. 'I have to admit that you are correct, Monsieur Smith, there is a Mme Esther Bolton at number seven Rue de Brive. Now I must act carefully while I await my orders. In the first place, you will

173

have to give me the name of someone who will vouch for you. And it must be someone in authority.'

Marianne held her breath. Who was there in the whole of this pitiful city who would vouch for Harvey? It was impossible, she was telling herself. But she was reckoning without the Harvey Burrage-Smith she was only just coming to know.

'Officer, I can assure you that Forster's Banking Company in the Rue St Denis will know that I have come from the English government to take Mrs Esther Bolton safely home. May we proceed?'

The officer, who had remained aloof during the whole of the conversation, suddenly became apopleptic and Marianne felt Harvey's grasp on her arm tighten as though in a warning.

'Proceed? Of course you may not proceed. You will both be kept in the jail until we have made our enquiries at the bank. Please don't waste any more of my time. I will send for guards to conduct you to the jail and there you will stay until I say otherwise.'

'And my carriage and horses, monsieur?'

If Marianne had not felt so desperately frightened, she would have laughed at Harvey's effrontery. Worrying about his carriage when threatened with jail and the possibility of the guillotine?

'You will be taken to the jail in your carriage and you will ride inside with your wife; the carriage will be kept there and your horses cared for until we know what is to happen to you. We French are not all the mob, the rabble, you English think us to be. True the horses would do well in a butcher's shop, but there is still the law and you have not been proved guilty yet. *Au revoir.*'

Politeness stopped then.

Frederic and Léon pushed Marianne back into the carriage and Harvey jumped in after her. The two guards took the driving seat, the gates were opened and they were off through the heaving mass which was Paris, towards the nearest jail.

Inside the carriage, Harvey held Marianne to him roughly and urgently.

'Marianne, you must listen to me. Do not think we have failed. I refuse to admit to failure. So be it, we are on our way to jail and you may be feeling that it is the end of it all. Look, my dear, I do not know if we will be kept together or if men and women are separated into different jails . . . what is it?' Harvey could tell that Marianne was struggling with her words and striving not to cry.

She moved closer to him, his very warmth

gave her courage. 'Harvey, I feel as though I can face anything as long as I am not parted from you. I expect the conditions in the jail will be horrifying, but if I have you near to me, I will be able to bear it.'

He kissed her. 'Marianne, if I am not there, you will be able to face it because you are a courageous person. We have not got this far only to be defeated.' The light in the carriage was dim, but he could see the frown on her face. 'Now, there is something else bothering you. Tell me.'

'I did not understand, Harvey. What you said about the bank. Did you make all that up or does it really give us any hope?'

'It does give us a shred of hope, my sweet. It was the only thing I could think of which might save us.'

'But how did you know the name and address like that, you sounded so confident when you told the officer.' Marianne was still puzzled, but Harvey kept nothing from her.

'I think I told you, Marianne. When I was asked by Lord Grenville to come for Esther Bolton, he said that the information of her situation had come from a messenger of Forster's in the Rue St Denis. All they could say was that Mr Bolton had gone to the guillotine and that his wife was being held captive at number seven Rue de Brive. What I said to the officer was the truth. Whether it will save us is another matter . . . hush, we are stopping.'

The door opened and Léon was shouting. 'Get out, the two of you, we are there.'

They were hustled out and the carriage led away. The building in front of them was formidable. A solid square of grey stone with no more than slits for windows, it was grimy with city soot and at the one main door they were greeted by four soldiers in red uniforms, rifles at the ready.

Marianne clung to Harvey's hand; her other hand clutched the bag she had packed in Sussex and which still contained Madame Franchot's bread and apples.

Harvey gave their names in a small office where two guards stood at the door. Afterwards, Marianne thought that it was the only room in the jail which was not dirty.

After that, she felt bewildered, but it comforted her that she had not been parted from Harvey. They were led along several narrow corridors before a turnkey opened a door for them and they were pushed inside a large room.

Marianne stood inside the room and felt as though the end of the world had come; only Harvey's hand on hers gave her any sense of reality.

There was very little light in the room, but there was enough for Marianne to be able to see a sorrowful mass of humanity lining the walls and sitting slumped over a rough table at the centre. All around the grey, cold walls was a rack; a mesh of metal covered with sacking and intended as a bed. Some were lying down, but tossing and turning in their restless state. Here and there she could catch a glimpse of a man or lady dressed decently as she and Harvey were; but for the most part, the inhabitants of that room were in rags, men in torn shirts, women in dresses which barely covered their shoulders.

Then there was the noise; a banging on the iron racks, a high, wretched wailing from the women, gruff and angry voices of the men, but worst of all were the cries of hungry children. What are children doing in this dreadful place, thought Marianne, with an ache in her heart and no thought to herself.

But the sights and sounds were bearable when compared to the stench of that room; the smell of unwashed human beings crowded together, the open drain which was the only sanitation; rot, filth and decay, and it filled Marianne's nostrils until she thought she would be sick.

'Sit over there,' they were told, 'and don't cause no trouble just because you're swells compared to most of what we've got here.'

They sat together on the rack, and Marianne put her arms right round Harvey's strong body; then his arms enfolded her and they were silent in their misery and their dilemma. They refused the mouldy bread which was brought to them and shared one of the apples from the bag, then Marianne lay against Harvey again.

'Do you think we are going to die, Harvey?' she asked him.

He hugged her. 'No, little one, I have a strange feeling of optimism and I am pinning my hopes on Forster's. Here we are in jail, Marianne, and now that we are incarcerated as Mr and Mrs Smith, I suppose that, once again, I will have to ask you to marry me.'

She raised her head and looked at him; he was quite serious. 'Oh, Harvey,' she said against his chest. 'I don't know whether to laugh or cry.' And she buried her face against him and wept until she fell asleep.

# 8

Marianne did not know how long she had slept and when she awoke, her first awareness was of Harvey's warmth against her.

Then the reality of the nightmare of their situation burst upon her as the sickening stench hit her stomach, and the cries and groans and weeping of the other prisoners came to her ears.

Harvey was still asleep and did not stir; it amazed her. She tried to guess what time it was, but could only tell that it was still the night as no glimmer of daylight penetrated the slits of windows high up in the roof.

Marianne afterwards thought that the loftiness of the room which was their jail was its only saving grace. In the light of the candles which were burning where the guards sat, she could look upwards and away from the degradation which surrounded her. She could see that the brickwork of the ceiling was formed in an intricate pattern which reminded her of the vaulting of an English cathedral.

In those early hours before Harvey stirred, her eyes lingered on the flickering light on the bricks and she tried to work out the pattern; she somehow felt herself saved from the madness of final despair. There must be some good in everything, she tried to tell herself. I still have Harvey's arms about me and I can look at the bricks in the roof. What a strange world, she thought, where in the midst of human misery, I can find beauty in a few bricks.

Light came at last and there was a crying restlessness about the inmates of that jail room; there was a hunger coupled with a realization that nothing had changed while they slept.

Harvey stirred at last. He looked at Marianne and she gave a little smile.

'Did I sleep?' he asked her. 'And why do you smile? There is nothing to smile about as I remember.'

'I am smiling because you are awake at last and because of the bricks.'

He looked at her sharply, worried lest she should be deranged.

'The bricks?'

She nodded. 'Yes, look at the roof; the bricks are placed in different patterns, it is fascinating. I have tried to work out the pattern and it has helped to pass the time while you slept.'

He looked upwards. 'Goddammit, you are

right; and you noticed it?' He looked at her. 'You are a remarkable girl, Marianne. My only thought is of food, I am hungry. Are you?'

'Everyone is hungry, Harvey. It is pitiful to hear the children crying. Look at that little family over there. Do you think that I should take them some of our bread? We have not touched the rolls which Mme Franchot gave us.'

His hand closed over hers, and he dared not tell her that those very children had possibly been put into the jail for stealing bread. 'I am sorry, Marianne, but I have to say no. Don't let the bread be seen. It would cause a riot and the very children you are trying to help will be hurt. Have patience, the warders will bring them something soon.'

But before the warders appeared with what would pass for breakfast, a guard in uniform opened the door and shouted out loud.

'Monsieur Smeet and his wife, please.'

Marianne felt Harvey stiffen. 'It is us,' he whispered.

'Here,' he called out and they stood up.

The guard walked over to them. 'Come with me.'

Almost in a dream, Marianne walked with Harvey down the same long corridors and into the small office at the front of the jail.

It was a different official this time, and
— Marianne thought — more senior.

'Mr Harvey Burrage-Smith?'

'Yes,' was all Harvey said and kept his hold
on Marianne's hand.

'I have orders to release you. Your
credentials at Forster's were excellent; they
were most generous and it is the order of the
Governor of the jail that you go and fetch the
young English woman from the Rue de Brive
and leave the country as soon as possible.
There will be no problems for you at the
North Gate.'

Harvey had not moved; he showed no
emotion and took Marianne by the arm.
'Thank you,' he said. 'And my carriage?'

Marianne marvelled at his audacity, but his
question was understood. 'It is at the front door.'

'Thank you,' said Harvey again. 'Come, my
dear.'

★   ★   ★

The carriage with its two horses was indeed
at the front of the jail, a boy holding the reins.
He gave a grin as Harvey reached into a
private pocket in the carriage and retrieved a
coin which he tossed to the lad. He helped
Marianne in, kissing her briefly and with a
smile.

'We are free, my dear, we are free and we will make haste to the Rue de Brive.'

'But, Harvey,' she protested. 'How was it we came to be released so quickly? Think of all those other poor wretches.'

'Money talks, dear girl,' he replied. 'Jailers are known to be corrupt, and the Governor will have received a goodly sum from Forster's for our release. They will have known just what to do, you can be sure, and we will find out from Mrs Bolton how they came to know of her predicament. Now we will go; you are comfortable?'

'Yes, thank you. I think I am a little dazed at being released from the jail, it all happened so suddenly and so quickly.'

For the rest of her life, Marianne was never to forget the scenes which greeted her on the streets of Paris as Harvey drove them through the city; she had noticed nothing when they were taken to the jail.

Harvey knew just where he had to go for he had been shown the map in London and he knew Paris well. Rue de Brive, no. 7.

But to get there, he had to go through the *faubourg* of St Antoine and then across the city and over the Pont Neuf. They passed through some handsome avenues with now leafless trees; some narrow streets, squalid and ill-smelling. And everywhere, the people;

the mass of the citizens of Paris, ill-dressed and dragging barely-clad children. Oh, the children, Marianne always remembered afterwards, half-starved and with dark sunken circles of hunger about their eyes.

Those crowds were all on the move and always to the same place. The same, crowded, noisy square where stood Madame Guillotine at her work; there were screams which were not of terror, but of joy as yet another aristocrat met his end.

Marianne could not drag her eyes away, yet she could look no more. Her teeth bit hard on her knuckles to stop the tears from coming. By the time they had crossed the Seine and Harvey was looking for the Rue de Brive, Marianne had sunk back in the carriage, sick and unable to cry, yet desperate to keep her senses so that she could help Harvey when he needed her.

At last, the carriage stopped and she heard Harvey jump down; his face appeared at the window, she thought he looked pale and drawn.

'Are you all right, Marianne? I am sorry to have brought you to such a Paris. It was once a beautiful place. I have not found the street and will have to ask directions . . . Marianne, are you sure that you are all right?'

At the kindness in his voice, the tears

started to roll down her cheeks. 'Give me your hand, Harvey, just for a second,' she said to him. 'I tried not to look, but I had to know what it was all about. Hunger everywhere, and blood. How could a country do this to itself? I know that a lot of the peasants were ill-used, but it was also many of the ordinary people who rebelled and this is the result. It is too horrible to contemplate. Now we must play our part in the tragedy. Please God we can get out alive.'

She was glad of his firm grip and felt his lips pressed into her palm. 'Courage, my dear girl, we will win through. You can trust your M. Carnot just as you trusted Mme Bézier. And you did remember to tell the guard that you were Mme Carnot. It was our misfortune that one of the guards came from Narbonne.'

'I did my best,' she whispered.

He squeezed her hand. 'We will win. But now I must ask directions to the Rue de Brive. I have a feeling that we are in the right *faubourg*, it cannot be far away.'

Marianne felt the carriage stop three times and voices at the front before Harvey set off at a more purposeful pace. Then they stopped and when she looked out of the window, she saw that they were in a mean street with small houses crowded closely together; the doors were shabby, the windows small and dirty.

Harvey appeared at the door of the carriage again. 'Number seven Rue de Brive, we have found it and I will tell you, Marianne, that I do not feel hopeful. There are a lot of people about and all dressed very poorly, without thick clothes to keep them warm in this weather. I cannot leave you alone in the carriage while I enquire at the house, we had better stay together. Let me help you down.'

Marianne jumped down beside him on to a road covered with muck and straw. Immediately they were surrounded by haggard, hungry faces and she realized that the warm mantle she had borrowed from her maid in England was as luxurious as the richest of fur coats here in France.

She saw that Harvey was thinking the same as herself for as they approached the door of no. 7, he threw a handful of coins as far as he could away from him. There was a clamour and a scrabble on the filthy road, but for the moment, the attention was taken from themselves.

Then Harvey sought for the tallest man in the crowd and called out to him. 'You there, monsieur, guard my horses for me. Here is a louis for you.'

He turned to the house and a sharp knock on the door brought an old lady; Marianne guessed her age to be about seventy years.

She had long grey hair and wore black; she stared at her visitors with fear in her eyes.

'I have done my best,' she said nervously.

Ignoring the strange remark, Harvey put a foot on the doorstep so that the door would not be closed against him.

'Who is it, Mère Didot?' a deep male voice called from behind her.

Harvey did not give her time to speak. 'It is Mr Burrage-Smith from England. I come seeking Mrs Esther Bolton. Is she here?'

A tall, rough man came to the door and stood behind the woman who was motionless. His speech was rough, too. 'Who is it asking for Mme Bolton?'

From the back of the house came a shrill scream and a cry and the man turned to the woman. 'Go and make sure that she doesn't run out, Ma.'

'You have a girl here then?' said Harvey. Marianne was clinging on to his hand for the scene had attracted the crowd and the two of them were pressed on all sides.

'Let me in,' demanded Harvey. 'I refuse to talk to you here.'

He gave the man a push, pulled Marianne in with him and they were inside a very small room with the door shut behind them.

'Now what's all this about?' blustered the big man.

'I am from the Foreign Office in England — here is my card — and I have been sent to search for Mrs Esther Bolton. We have received intelligence that she is at this address.' Harvey paused and looked around him. The room, though small, was surprisingly clean and tidy, the only furniture being a table and four wooden chairs and — more surprising — a small bookcase full of tattered volumes. 'Now tell me who you are, if you please; who is the old woman and who was it we heard crying out in the back? I might as well add that you be well rewarded for your cooperation.'

'You mean money?' asked the man, a look of greed in his eyes.

'I mean money. Your name?'

A second's hesitation and then Harvey took a cloth bag of coins from his pocket, rattled it and put it back in his pocket again.

'I am Georges Lemarc, I am a guard. I was chosen, because of my strength to watch over a certain young English lady.'

'And the woman?'

'She is Mère Didot, she is a widow and her husband was a scholar though a poor man, you see his books. Her memory is bad, she cannot read, but she is kindly and she can cook. I am given money for meat and bread and Mme Bolton has helped; we survive better than the poorer people outside.'

'And the name of the English woman?'

'Mme Esther Bolton.'

Marianne gave a cry, but Harvey held her back. 'Fetch her, please, Georges Lemarc, and for your sake, I hope that she is well.'

Georges opened the inside door of the room and Marianne could see that beyond was a small scullery. 'Mme Esther,' he called. 'Come here at once; and you, Mère Didot.'

The old woman came first followed by a young girl who stood in the doorway. Marianne thought that she was the most beautiful young lady she had ever seen. She was dressed plainly in dark blue and was at once seen to be dainty and neat; but it was her hair and her eyes which proclaimed her beauty. It was immediately evident that her long fair hair had been kept clean during her imprisonment in the small house, for it fell to her shoulders in shining curls. The features of her face were small, even and unremarkable, but her blue eyes were large and beautiful — and at that moment, desperately sad. She looked confused and stared first at Marianne and then at Harvey.

'Who . . . who are you?' she stammered.

Harvey went quietly up to her, but did not

touch her. 'I am Mr Harvey Burrage-Smith and I come from the English Foreign Office. If you can prove that you are indeed Mrs Esther Bolton, we will try and smuggle you back to England. We are sorry to hear of your tragic loss and of your misfortune . . . '

'I don't believe it,' she cried out and threw herself into Harvey's arms. He held her while she sobbed and stroked her hair gently.

Marianne, watching them, felt an almost unbelievable sense of jealousy, but she made no move.

At last, Harvey spoke. 'Mrs Bolton, please come and sit down and I want you to meet Marianne. She is Miss Marianne Welford and she has come with me — posing as my wife — so that you will have a female companion.'

Esther Bolton walked past Harvey into the room; she went up to Marianne and took her hands. 'I shall call you Marianne; to think that I thought that I should never see an English face again. You are very kind.' Her voice was now composed and quiet and Marianne put her arms around her and kissed her cheek.

'I am glad we have found you,' she said quietly.

Georges stood at the street door leaving Esther to sit at the table with Harvey and

Marianne. Mme Didot remained out of sight in the scullery.

'Can you tell us what has happened?' Harvey asked. 'Or is it too painful for you?'

Esther shook her head. 'No, I will be glad to talk to you, but I do not understand how you can get me back to England. We will speak in English and it will be safer for neither Georges nor Mme Didot speak any English. They have not been unkind to me. Georges is obeying orders and I think that Mme Didot has a kind heart; she even washed my hair for me . . . but are we really going to escape . . . what about Georges?'

'He can be bribed and we have a small carriage outside; we will wait until it is getting dark and there are not so many people in the streets. While we are waiting, can you tell us what has happened?'

Esther Bolton placed both hands on the table as though it would give her support; Harvey stretched out and covered her hands with one of his, and so they remained throughout the recital.

'It is a long story,' she began, 'and I don't know if I will get it all in the right order. Do you know anything about it at all? Charles and myself, I mean.'

'Nothing; only that he was at Forster's and had been taken, also that you were a captive.'

192

'I don't know if I can tell you without crying, but I will try hard. Yes, Charles was a banker and worked for Forster's; sometimes in London, sometimes in Paris. We have been here for two years and they were worrying and dreadful times, but we thought that being English, we were safe. We rented a nice house in Rue Berger, not far from the bank . . . I am sorry, I must get to the point.'

'No, please take your time,' Harvey told her and his tone was kind. Marianne could see that he was watching the girl's face closely.

'It was early one morning, but after breakfast. Charles was preparing to go to the bank when the front door was burst open and three men stood there. I was terrified for through the open door, I could see the tumbrel — you know what a tumbrel is? It was standing in the street outside the house. The leader of the men just laughed and said 'Charles Bolton, your turn for Madame la Guillotine'.

'Then they turned to me. 'A carriage awaits you, madame,' they said in a nasty way.

'I tried to cling to Charles, but the three of them were very strong and they took him . . . just like that. In seconds, he was gone and I could only stand there and watch the tumbrel going up the street. Then everything seemed to turn hazy and black and the next minute, there was a guard back at the door — it was Georges, as it happened. He took my arm and led me to a small carriage. 'Where are we going?' I asked him, I dared not think of Charles.

''To number seven Rue de Brive,' he replied. 'You will be my prisoner until it is your turn.'

'I tried to think clearly, but it was impossible, though I did manage to pick up my mantle. I felt very sick and dizzy, but I did remember Forster's — if the guard would take me there, I could leave a message to send to England. So I said to Georges with all the strength I could muster, 'Take me to Forster's, I must have money.'

'He looked at me and said, 'You will give me money?' and I replied, yes, of course I would. All the time I was trying not to think of Charles. It was not far to the bank and Georges took me to the door, but he did not come in as he was keeping an eye on the carriage. When I saw Charles's colleagues, I started to cry, but although they were upset, they understood and gave me some money; then they made me sit down and write a message which they would send to England. My hand was shaking, but I did manage to write a few words which I hoped would make sense.'

*Charles taken to guillotine. I am captive at number seven Rue de Brive. Please help me.*
    *Esther Bolton*

'I managed to give it to them just as Georges came back into the bank for me. I pushed a louis into his hand and said 'I am ready'.'

Esther Bolton stopped speaking and looked at them. 'I am sorry that it took so long in the telling, but I wanted you to know everything. It means that they did receive my message in England for you have come. How can I ever thank you? I have not been badly treated here and the money did help. But I feel numb, I feel as though I am in a dream and will wake up and Charles will be there. I cannot believe that he has gone in just a few seconds like that.'

Harvey kept his hold on her hands. 'You don't know why they came for him?'

Esther shook her head. 'He was English, but I don't think it was that. He tended to be too outspoken. He did not agree with the Revolution. He agreed that change was needed, but that mob violence was not the way of ruling a country. That is the kind of thing he would say to me, and if he spoke those same words outside, then he would have been under suspicion. I am afraid I used

195

to tell him to try and be careful, but he would laugh and say that being an employee at Forster's would ensure his safety from the guillotine . . . ' Her face crumpled and tears filled her eyes. 'I am sorry . . . I still cannot believe that he has gone . . . and you are so good to come for me.'

Marianne put an arm around the shaking shoulders and met Harvey's eyes across the fair hair. The message in his expression was — *we will do our best for her.*

Mère Didot cooked them a splendid dinner of mutton and vegetables which Georges — with plenty of money in his pocket — had walked a long way to the market to purchase.

As soon as the light began to fade, they could hear from inside the small room that the crowds were dispersing to whatever shelter they had for the night.

Harvey made sure that the carriage was still there and gave the man another louis for his efforts. He asked where he could get feed for the horses, but the man shook his head and Harvey went back to ask Georges who, sensing that more money might come his way, offered to take Harvey to the Marché de la Cité where they would be able to buy oats.

All this took time, and when they finally left the Rue de Brive and thanked Mère

Didot as they said goodbye, it was almost dark.

Harvey managed to find his way back to the North Gate with Marianne and Esther sitting very close together in the carriage. Esther was shivering in spite of her mantle, but she did not cry.

Marianne put her arms around the girl to try and keep her warm. 'Try not to be frightened, Esther,' she said. 'You have been through a terrible ordeal, but Harvey knows what he is about. One day perhaps I will be able to tell you how he came into France dressed as an old farm woman and brought my French cousins safely to us in Susssex.'

'You live in Sussex, Marianne? Is that where we will go now?'

Marianne nodded. 'Yes, I hope so, but first we have to get past the North Gate. On our way to fetch you, we went wrong there and had to spend a night in jail before we came to the Rue de Brive.'

'You went to jail for me? There is no end to your kindness, but — '

'Hush, Esther,' Marianne said quickly. 'I can hear voices and I think we must be arriving at the gate. In fact, if I am not mistaken, I can hear laughter which seems very strange. Can you see anything out of the window on your side?'

'Harvey has jumped down from the driving seat, and he is talking to two of the guards. They are laughing at him, that is what you can hear. Do you want to have a look?'

But before Marianne could lean across the carriage to look out of the window, the guard who called himself Léon had opened the door and was standing there.

'Mesdames, it is my pleasure; please to get out of the carriage. I have been talking to the so-called Monsieur Carnot who turned out to be an Englishman and went to the jail for his sins.'

He helped them both out and seemed polite. They could see that Harvey was having an argument with the other guard who was a stranger to them.

Marianne held Esther's hand and listened carefully.

The guard's voice was strident. 'Very well, you are Mr Burrage-Smith and this is your wife and you take Mme Bolton to England. But how do we know that you have the permission? One day, the officer on duty sends you to the jail, the next day, you tell us you are to leave the country. We have no authority to let you go, I think it will be back to the jail for you, monsieur.'

Harvey's expression did not change and Marianne held on to Esther; she could not believe that this very scene was happening all over again. Not the jail again, please God, not the jail again, she kept saying to herself.

'Your superior officer is here?' Harvey asked curtly.

'He is here, but he is busy. A whole family from Paris are here and say that they only want to go as far as Compiègne. But why, we ask them? Their old mother is ill, she might not live until the morning, that is their story; so we send them to the officer, he will decide. And, monsieur, only he can decide your case.'

'I may talk to my wife and our companion?' Harvey asked.

'Of course, monsieur, we are not heartless. Léon and myself, we do only our duty.'

Harvey walked towards the two girls and put his arm around Esther. 'Do not be afraid, Esther, we were promised a safe passage out of Paris by the governor of the jail. Forster's were very generous and I am afraid that in this dreadful time of ours, money will buy everything.'

'It did not save Charles,' said Esther tearfully and she turned to Marianne, who gave the girl a hug and looked reproachfully at Harvey.

But Harvey had turned away from them as a family came hurrying out of the guards' office followed by the officer on duty.

Marianne's heart sank. It was the same man who had sent them to the jail the night before.

'Ha, Monsieur Smith; Monsieur Burrage-Smith, I think I should say. You are back already? You must have spoken a kind word in the governor's ear. I wonder why I have not heard from him?'

Marianne saw a stony look cross Harvey's face. 'I was assured at the jail that the governor wished us back in England as soon as possible; that there would be no problem for us at the North Gate. Have you looked through your papers, monsieur?'

The air between them was fraught. 'You dare to question my efficiency, Monsieur Smith? *Sapristi*, I think it will be the jail for another night and for three of you this time, it seems.'

'Monsieur.' Harvey's tone changed to one of flattery and persuasion and Marianne thought him wise. 'You run the affairs of the North Gate very efficiently, your guards are well-trained and they are not impolite. I congratulate you. But may I respectfully suggest that the note from the governor which was issued early this morning might well be lying at the bottom of the pile of correspondence which you have received today? Might I ask that you have a look for it?

It is more for the sake of my wife and and this young English lady than for myself that I ask you this.'

The officer looked at Marianne and then at Esther before turning and speaking to Harvey.

'Wait there if you please, while I go into my office,' he said and strode off, his head held stiffly, his step deliberate.

Not a word was said at the gate, and being late evening, no more carriages or wagons waited to be let through.

Marianne stood with her hand clutching Esther's; Harvey was near them, his hand still on Esther's shoulder.

Marianne thought that it seemed like an eternity before the officer came back; his expresson had not changed, but he was holding a small card in his hand.

'It is no more than a card of the governor's with a message on it; small wonder that I missed it. I will read it to you.'

OFFICER OF THE NORTH GATE
*Let M. Burrage-Smith and company pass without delay.*

'And then his initials; that is all, but it is good enough for me. I wish you a safe return to England.'

Esther burst into tears and Harvey helped her into the carriage. Marianne jumped in after her and did her best to comfort the stricken girl.

'It has all been too much for you, Esther, but we are safe now.'

She looked up at Harvey who was still standing at the carriage door and she could see that his eyes were full of concern for Esther.

'I am glad that you are here, Marianne, I was right to bring you,' he said. 'Look, my dear girls, it is nearly dark and there is no moon. I do not know the road well enough to reach Dieppe tonight. So I plan to drive as far as Pontoise; it is only a few miles north of Paris and will have a good inn. It will be better for us to sleep there and make an early start for Dieppe in the morning.'

Marianne was grateful for his thoughtfulness and she smiled. 'Thank you, Harvey, and Esther will be glad of my company.'

The guards said farewell and unlocked the gates; Harvey drove off and Marianne told Esther what the plan was.

'I will never be able to thank you,' Esther said, 'and it is kind of Harvey to give us a night's rest before our journey to England. I will try not to cry again, Marianne.'

The road was quiet and they were

approaching Pontoise in what seemed a very short space of time. At a small inn, they obtained rooms for the night, with the two girls sharing a modest bedroom, but with a bed each.

Although it was late, a substantial supper was served to them; they ate in silence.

Harvey took the girls upstairs and wished them goodnight, kissing both of them on the cheek before going to his own room which was along the corridor.

Warm bricks had been put in the beds and both Marianne and Esther had no hesitation in sleeping in their chemises, spreading their dresses over the ends of the beds.

They said but few words as both of them were tired, but Marianne sensed immediately that Esther had not settled down and was trying to hide her sobs.

Marianne sat up. 'Esther, please don't cry, would you like to talk to me?'

Esther's head was buried in her pillow, but Marianne could hear the muffled reply. 'I shall never sleep. It is Charles, Marianne, it is Charles. I shall never see him again. I think the real truth has only just come to me.'

Marianne did not hesitate. She got out of her own bed, picked up the counterpane to wrap around herself and sat by Esther's side, putting her arms round the girl until the sobs had ceased.

# 9

Sitting on Esther's bed, Marianne propped the pillows up and spoke to her kindly but firmly. 'Try not to cry, Esther, it will make you weak. I will stay here and you can sit up and talk to me. Tell me something of yourself, I know nothing about you. Can you bear to speak to me of Charles?'

Esther did as she was told, but she was still tearful. 'It has only just come to me that I will never see Charles again. All that time at Mère Didot's, it seemed as though he had gone off and was coming back to fetch me. I think it must be the fact that we have left Paris behind us and I am with you and Harvey, and not with Charles. The real truth has suddenly hit me.'

Marianne thought that she had better find out if Esther had any family in England before she said anything else.

'Can you go to your parents in England, Esther?' she asked.

The question opened floodgates, but afterwards, Marianne thought that it was the best thing she could have done.

'I have no parents, Marianne. They both

died when I was little and I was brought up by an aunt of mine, my father's sister. She is Lady Peddar and she lives in London, I call her Aunt Florence. She was widowed when she was quite young and had no children; I always had the feeling that taking her brother's child into her home had been an imposition to her. She went about frequently in fashionable circles as she had been left in wealthy circumstances by her husband.'

'You do not like her, Esther,' observed Marianne.

'No, no, I must not say that. She did everything for me; the best governesses she could find, the finest clothes and everything of the latest fashion. But, you see, although she was kind to me in all these things, she showed me no affection whatsoever. I was for ten years like a stranger in the house.'

'What happened then?'

The voice which had been speaking quite firmly suddenly faltered, then stopped altogether.

'Try, Esther. Was that when you met Charles?'

Esther nodded. 'I was given a splendid come-out when I was eighteen and I met Charles at my ball. He was older than me for he was nearly twenty-six, but we fell in love, Marianne. Just like that, it was so romantic.

Aunt Florence approved of Charles — I think she would have approved of any gentleman who would take me off her hands.' She broke off. 'Oh dear, that is not a very nice thing to say when I should be so grateful to her. But Charles worked at Forster's and travelled between London and Paris, so he was regarded as a suitable husband for me. We were married a year later and we rented a house in Paris; that was two years ago and, of course, they have been wicked times in France. We did not feel safe, but Charles thought that his position at the bank would give us some protection . . . '

'You spoke French, Esther?'

The girl nodded. 'Yes, I did. It was one of the things Aunt Florence insisted on and I had a mamselle for a year; I liked the language and by the time I met Charles, I could speak fluent French. I think it was one of the things which made us so close in the beginning . . . ' she stopped and looked at Marianne. 'Do you know, Marianne, I think it is doing me good to tell you all about it. I know that Charles is . . . dead . . . but nothing can take away those happy two years, can they?'

Marianne leaned over and kissed the girl's cheek. 'I think that you are very brave and whatever happens in the future, you will always have that time to look back on.'

But she had said the wrong thing for a cloud of worry came into Esther's eyes. 'Marianne, I cannot face going to live with Aunt Florence again. I know she is a good woman, but she is not kind like you and Harvey. You are lucky to be married to him . . . no, that is wrong, is it not? He said that you were only posing as his wife for safety's sake. Are you going to marry him?'

Marianne shook her head. Was she going to marry Harvey, she wondered, when this masquerade was over? 'I was betrothed to him once, but we quarrelled, so I do not know what is going to happen now. Never mind about me, where will you go, Esther, if you refuse to go back to your aunt?'

'I don't know, I cannot think of it,' came the forlorn reply.

Marianne tried to be cheerful. 'Then we will not think of it. You can come back to Welford Grange with me and you can stay for just as long as you wish. You can go riding with Harvey, if you like.'

Marianne saw Esther smile for the first time and it was a sweet smile. 'You mean that you will lend him to me? There is no limit to your kindness, Marianne, but I won't steal Harvey from you!'

They laughed then and Marianne made

Esther lie down to try and get off to sleep. The talk had done them both good, and being warm and comfortable, and very tired, they slept soundly.

Next morning, they were given a good breakfast and Harvey was handing them into the carriage before it was light.

After that, all went smoothly. They reached Dieppe with no difficulties for the road was quiet at that hour. Harvey exchanged the carriage for the wagon, and at the West Gate of the town, the guard was missing. Then there was nothing to stop them reaching St Pierre-sur-Mer in good time.

Mme Franchot told them that the *Marie Rose* appeared each morning and afternoon, but did not linger when it became obvious that the passengers had not yet reached the coast.

Marianne made Harvey take Esther for a walk along the sands and he seemed pleased to perform the task. Esther is very taken with Harvey in spite of her grief over Charles, there is no question about it, Marianne was thinking as she watched them set off, and Harvey is taken with Esther. I must be glad for them both.

They sailed to Newhaven in the early afternoon and as soon as they were taken off the *Marie Rose*, Harvey sent a boy to Welford

Grange with a message. Sir Thomas arrived before darkness had fallen, and dinner-time found the two girls back at Welford Grange. They bathed and changed into clean clothes and it was fortunate that Esther was very much the same build as Lucy and was easily suited with underclothes and a dress of warm velveteen of their favourite blue.

In the company of Marianne and Lucy — still awaiting Edouard's return — it was easy to keep Esther from a fit of the dismals. Harvey had declined the invitation to stay and had ridden back to Broadoaks telling them that he would come again in the morning.

After dinner, Marianne sat with her father in the library and told him of their experiences.

He looked grave. 'You have done very well, my dear. It would have worried me if I had thought that you would be put into jail, but now that you have arrived home with Esther, I must not regret sending you to France.'

'You will not object if Esther stays here for a little while, Papa? She is very reluctant to live with her aunt in London. It seems that Lady Peddar is not a very caring person.'

His reply was instant and generous. 'Esther can make her home here if she so wishes. I still have hopes of you and Harvey, and I can sense that Esther and Lucy will become attached to one another. Lucy seems to be pining for Edouard and Esther will be good company for her. I would be very pleased to be able to offer Esther a home with us.'

Marianne kissed him on the cheek. 'Thank you, Papa, you are very good to us.'

It seemed that Sir Thomas's prophecy about Esther and Lucy was correct, for when Marianne returned to the drawing-room, it was to find the two girls deep in conversation about Charles and Edouard.

Esther was shown over the house and given her own bedroom; more tears were shed as she said goodnight to Marianne, but this time, they were as much tears of gratitude as of sadness.

'I cannot begin to thank you, Marianne, and your father, too.' Esther looked very tired, but Marianne thought that the girl's expression was almost cheerful which, under the circumstances, seemed strange.

That was until she heard Esther's next words. 'Marianne, I was telling Lucy how I was feeling and I would like to say the same to you. It is rather odd, you will think, but I have this feeling that Charles is not far away. That he is thinking of me and trying to reach me. I know that you will consider that I am being silly, but I find it very comforting.'

Marianne found herself at a loss for words and it was not easy to make a suitable reply. 'Esther, we know that Charles had died, but we believe that the soul lives on into eternity; it may be that his spirit watches over you. Can you believe that?'

But Esther was shaking her head. 'No, it is not like that. It just feels that he is not far away, that I have not really lost him.'

Marianne thought it best to let the girl think such thoughts. It is early days, she said silently to herself, let Esther believe that now, it will comfort her. Later on, she will be stronger and will be able to come to terms with the truth. She is young and very pretty and will probably marry again; and unbidden into Marianne's mind, came the thought of Harvey and it came with a sense of uneasiness.

Harvey rode over from Broadoaks the next day as promised and Marianne watched as Esther went up to him and took his hand; he looked down at the young widow with a fond expression in his eyes. Marianne knew that she should be grateful.

Within minutes of his arrival and before they had decided whether to ride or walk out, a carriage was drawn up at the front of Welford Grange and with shrieks of joy from Lucy, they saw Edouard walking towards the front door. He wore a long topcoat of deep navy blue and he carried a tricorne; in the drawing-room, his coat removed, he greeted Lucy fondly and was introduced to Esther.

'My parents send their kindest regards,' he said to Sir Thomas who had come into the drawing-room on hearing the commotion. 'And I think that Annette is hoping for a visit from Luke when he comes down from Oxford for Christmas. We are very settled in our London home.'

He turned to Lucy who was trying to behave with some decorum when it was obvious to all that the only thing she wanted to do was to throw herself into Edouard's arms.

'Lucy, will you walk in the garden with me? I need to talk to you privately,' he said to her.

Lucy flushed with pleasure and glanced at her father; she was a great favourite with him and he nodded indulgently. He guessed that he would be asked for an interview by Edouard on their return and did not seem to think it amiss that Edouard should speak to Lucy first. He was not a gentleman for strict formality or obedience to etiquette.

Lucy ran upstairs to fetch her pelisse and bonnet, and the day being cold, Edouard picked up his topcoat again.

As soon as they were out of the front door,

he took her hand and she smiled up at him; but her smile fell away when she saw that his expression was very serious.

'What is it, Edouard?' she asked anxiously. 'There is something that does not please you, yet you have asked me to come out here with you privately. I have been so impatient, I longed to see you again since our last meeting.'

He took her hands and turned her towards him. 'I am a brute to bring you out on this cold day, is there nowhere we can find shelter from the wind?'

She pointed across the gardens at the front of the house. 'In the corner of the rose garden . . . look. There is the summer house, or that is what we always called it when we were children; it has no door, but there is a seat and we would be sheltered.'

'Just the thing,' he said quietly and they walked across the garden and sat together in the small wooden shelter.

'It is covered with honeysuckle in the summer,' Lucy told him.

Edouard turned to her, and untied the strings of her bonnet, tipping it back on her head. 'I want to see if you are as pretty as I remembered,' he said, dropping a light kiss on to not unwilling lips.

'Have you brought good news with you,

Edouard?' she asked him, then, seeing his heavy frown, wished she had not spoken.

'I have to tell you, Lucy, that although I love you dearly, I cannot ask your father for his permission to marry you . . . there, I have upset you. I did not mean to be as blunt as that. Would you like to be married to me?'

Lucy gave a slight nod. 'Yes, Edouard, I would like it very much. I thought you would say something to Papa before you went back to London or that you would write to him.'

'I am sorry, Lucy, I find myself at a pass, as you would say over here. I am Le Vicomte d'Amand, but in this country, I am nothing. Our London home is comfortable but small; there would be no room for myself and a new wife. My father is a good man and invested enough money in this country for our immediate needs, but that did not include the support of my wife and family. I needed my own career, my own residence before I could say anything to you.'

'But you have found nothing?' she asked in a small voice.

'Nothing.' His voice was flat, full of a defeat which hit Lucy as forcefully as if he had struck her. 'I could not write it all in a letter, so I decided I must come and see you. You are just as beautiful as I remember you to be and I want to go down on my knees in this little summer house and beg you to marry me. But I cannot.'

He pulled her against him then and Lucy knew the urgency of passion for the first time in her young life; his hands slipped under her pelisse, his lips roamed her face before finding hers. They clung together in desperation and in love.

Lucy broke away at last. Her heart was beating and she was sensible enough to know that such conduct was forbidden to her; she also knew that she was going to speak to Edouard as a young lady should never speak.

'I love you, Edouard, there is no one else for me; and I would marry you no matter how humble a position you held in life. Tell me what you have tried.'

'I did study at the Sorbonne, but I read only the classics. That fits me to be a schoolmaster and little else, but I cannot offer you such a poor life. If I had read for the law, it would have been a different matter. I could join the army, but would it be the English or the French army? We are at war . . . bah, it is impossible. The Foreign Office would not have me because I am French, our own embassy is out of the question. I have tried everything, Lucy, *ma chérie*, there is nothing for me to do but to live at home with my father and mother until we can return to

France. There is only one glimmer of light, but it means asking you to wait for me and I don't know how long it would be.'

'I would wait for you, Edouard,' said Lucy eagerly.

He kissed her again.

'My father has a country estate at Belfort and I was learning the management of it before the troubles started in France. If we waited, I could take you there, but it is too uncertain; not one of us knows what the outcome of the Revolution will be.'

'Have you any money at all, Edouard? I am sorry if it is impertinent of me to ask!'

He laughed then. 'You can ask me anything you like, Lucy! Yes, I do have a little investment left to me by my grandfather; it is in a London bank, but it would not be enough for us to live on.'

'Could you not rent a house in London and start a school yourself? You are educated and I am sure that you would make a good schoolmaster. It would be somewhere for us to live and I could cook a luncheon for your pupils!'

She found herself enfolded in his arms and her bonnet fell to the ground, his lips were on her hair.

'I love you, Lucy Welford. You are not only beautiful, you are a young lady of much character and fortitude. Lucy, I will say this to you: I will think about it. The last place I can imagine myself is in a school, but I will go back to London and talk it over with my father. Will that satisfy you for the time being? Are you willing to wait a little longer?'

She nodded. 'I would wait forever, Edouard. Now let us go back and tell Marianne; I have always told her everything and she is so sensible.'

He stood up and helped her on with her bonnet. 'That is a very good suggestion,' he told her and they walked quickly back to the house.

Marianne's eyes searched their faces as they came into the drawing-room and she could see, not joy, but a happy determination about them. It puzzled her somewhat; she had expected radiance or tears.

Harvey was with them and was engaged in a light-hearted chatter with Esther.

Marianne had been watching them together; Harvey seems to have the gift of cheering Esther up, she said to herself and found that her thoughts were not charitable.

Edouard told them of the plan and Marianne listened without interrupting him. At last, she gave her opinion and feared that she was going to cast gloom on their hopes.

'It is a solution to your problem,' she said

quietly, 'but I can't somehow see either of you as a schoolmaster and his wife. There *are* selective private academies, but they are usually run by middle-aged spinsters who teach not much more than music and needlework . . . no, I am not making it up so you need not laugh at me. An aristocratic, handsome French vicomte hardly fits the role of schoolmaster.'

Lucy looked downhearted. 'You don't think that it is a good venture, Marianne?' she asked her sister.

Marianne shook her head. 'No, I am not saying that; it is very courageous. The best idea is for Edouard to talk it over with his father, as he says. My cousin is the best person to ask for advice in these things.'

She watched as Edouard and Lucy joined Harvey and Esther and leaving them all talking eagerly, she thoughtfully sought out her father in the library.

Sir Thomas listened to her tale carefully; she saw him frown a little, then nod his head and finally, make his comment. 'Thank you for coming to tell me, Marianne. I believe the two of them to be sincerely attached and I think that Edouard would make a good husband for Lucy. But a school? I think not. Leave it to me, my dear, I have an idea and I will think it over and speak to Edouard later.'

Marianne felt satisfied as she left her father; she arrived back in the drawing-room in time to say farewell to Harvey, who said that he would come again in the morning and if it was a brighter day, perhaps they could all go riding together.

Dinner over, Edouard joined Sir Thomas for their glass of port and was all prepared to ask permission to address himself to Lucy and to speak of the plans for their livelihood; but before the question was posed, Sir Thomas announced his intention of wanting to speak seriously about Edouard's future.

'Edouard, I believe it to be true that you and my daughter, Lucy, have become attached to one another, but that you would have difficulty in providing for her.'

'Yes, that is true, Cousin Thomas, I wished to speak to you about it.'

'Just wait a moment, my boy, for I have a proposition to put to you. It has been a concern of mine for some little time and I think that your wish to marry Lucy might help me out of a quandary.'

Edouard looked surprised, but did not interrupt.

'Let me explain; you may not know the ways of the English peerage. I am a baronet and my eldest son will one day inherit my title; of course, that is your cousin Luke. I think that day will be some time off as I am not an old man and hope to have many years remaining to me. I have a substantial estate here in Sussex and have been pleased to manage it myself; I am a countryman and do not enjoy the pursuits of the city. My land is my life, you might say. You understand all this? I am taking a long time to come to the point.'

Edouard nodded. 'Certainly, cousin.'

Sir Thomas continued. 'It has been in my mind recently that although I enjoy the management of the estate, it is time that I had someone younger to go round the farms for me and gradually take up the position of my steward as I become older. Naturally, I have always thought that it would be Luke, but Luke has refused. The work does not interest him, and he is determined on going into politics when he leaves Oxford. You begin to see the drift of my meaning?'

'I ... I am not sure,' half-stammered Edouard as a gleam of unbelievable light showed itself.

'If it is your wish to marry Lucy and you have no position in the country, then I would like to ask you if you would be willing to take up the reins of Welford Grange by becoming my steward. You and Lucy, of course, would be able to make the Grange your home

— there is enough room here for two or three families.' Sir Thomas paused with a smile. 'I have surprised you. Go away and think about it, talk it over with Lucy. Then if both of you are agreeable, take Lucy up to London and ask your father his opinion. Is that fair?'

Edouard rose, reached across the library desk and shook Sir Thomas by the hand. 'I am overwhelmed,' he said and could not hide his enthusiasm. 'I must tell you, cousin, that I had already started to learn the ways of management at the de Charnay estate in Belfort. I would not be coming to you completely inexperienced. I will never be able to show my gratitude, except by hard work, of course. May I go and tell Lucy?'

Sir Thomas was all smiles. 'Yes, of course, off you go . . . oh, and Edouard, I expect you have already asked Lucy to marry you, but I give my permission.'

In the drawing-room, they were all talking at once at Edouard's news. Marianne smiled, Lucy cried and Esther looked on with a wistful happiness for them.

Edouard kissed Lucy in front of them all. 'Will you marry me, Lucy? You will be able to go on living at Welford Grange, your papa says that we can have our own apartment. Oh, and he also said that I had his permission to ask you to marry me.'

Lucy kissed Edouard shyly. 'He is the dearest father that ever was, I must go to him.'

She ran to the library and cried again as she hugged her father. 'Thank you, Papa, thank you. I am so happy and you must come into the drawing-room and ask for a bottle of champagne to be sent up from the cellar. We will have a celebration.'

The celebration went on for quite a long time and it was planned that Edouard would take Lucy back to London the very next morning.

It so happened that Marianne and Esther waved Edouard's carriage off before Harvey arrived; when he did come, he was delighted with the news.

Each morning after that, Harvey rode over to Welford Grange and insisted on accompanying Marianne and Esther on a walk through the park, or, if the ground was not too hard, they would ride out, sometimes as far as Lewes.

Marianne soon discovered that Esther, in spite of being brought up in London and living for two years in Paris, was very fond of riding.

Marianne also discovered that Esther was coming close to idolizing Harvey.

Harvey Burrage-Smith, for reasons known

only to himself, was being very kind to Esther. He made her talk to him about Charles, he teased her, he sometimes held her by the hand when talking to her.

Marianne watched it all, and as each day passed by, she knew that she was becoming jealous. Harvey did not neglect her, but each time he showed a special kindness to Esther, Marianne felt a twist to her heart. Harvey belongs to me, she would tell herself, then knew only too well that she had cast him off.

Then they had a further spat — it could not be called a quarrel — one morning when Harvey arrived to find Marianne already around at the stables.

It was a sunny morning and crisply inviting. Marianne knew that Harvey would want to ride; she was giving the orders for the saddling of the horses for herself and Esther.

'Marianne,' Harvey greeted her cheerily as he dismounted. 'You guessed that I would want to ride; are your horses saddled?'

'They will be in a few minutes,' she replied.

'Is Esther ready? Shall I go and see?'

'You can if you so wish,' Marianne replied primly and immediately regretted her tone.

'What is this?' he asked and he was smiling at her. 'You sound very stiff. Have I offended you? Not jealous because of my attentions to Esther, are you?'

223

Marianne was cross because she knew very well that this was so, but admit it, she would not. 'Of course I am not jealous. You are quite free to bestow your affections where you choose.'

He was standing close to her and put a finger under her chin. 'I will have you know, Miss Marianne Welford, that I bestow my affections — as you so aptly put it — on Esther because I feel very sorry for her. And if you feel jealous then I think it pleases me; but we will not go into that now or we will find ourselves in disagreement with each other.'

'I don't wish to quarrel with you again, Harvey.'

'We can't quarrel, my sweet, I am going to kiss you.'

'Harvey . . . ' Marianne started to say as she felt his hand move from her chin to the back of her head in order to draw her face closer to him. But his lips had stopped her words as, once again, Marianne experienced the passion of Harvey's kiss.

He seemed reluctant to draw away, and kept an arm round her shoulders to lead her to the house in search of Esther. 'Very nice, my dear Marianne, I enjoyed the kiss, we must do it more often . . . ah, here is Esther.'

He coolly took Esther's hands and they all returned to the stables for their mounts. A gallop towards Lewes was enjoyed, but Marianne did not forget the strange behaviour of Mr Harvey Burrage-Smith . . . or his kiss.

★  ★  ★

It was four days after Edouard and Lucy had left for London that Esther went missing.

The day had started wet and Marianne and Esther did not expect Harvey. They sat together in the drawing-room and Marianne noticed that Esther seemed quiet and sad that morning. She began to wonder if it was because it was too wet for Harvey to ride over to see them.

'You are very quiet this morning, Esther. Are you not feeling well?'

'I am quite well, thank you, Marianne, but I have it on my mind that I must write to my Aunt Florence in London. I should have done it before this, but I have been putting it off. I must tell her about Charles . . . it is not easy.' She broke off and looked up; Marianne saw that there were tears in her eyes. 'I have to tell my aunt that Charles is dead when I cannot believe it myself . . . ' She got to her feet, the tears were now streaming down her cheeks. 'I cannot believe it, Marianne. It cannot be true, it just can't be true . . . oh, what shall I do?'

And with these last words lost in her sobs, she ran out of the room and Marianne heard the fierce bang of the front door as Esther left the house.

'Oh, poor Esther.' Marianne said the words out loud. 'She has run out in the rain; I will go after her with a shawl or a cloak.'

She found two heavy shawls in the cloaks cupboard and put one round herself as she ran out after Esther. She looked around, but there was no sign of any running figure. I don't know which way to go after her, she was thinking. I suppose that the summer house is the best place to try.

But Marianne found that the summer house was empty and by this time she was getting very wet, so she made her way quickly back to the house not knowing what to do next. As she reached the front door, the sound of horses hoofs and wheels on the gravel made her turn round and she recognized Harvey's carrriage.

He saw her and jumped down.

'Whatever are you doing out in the rain, Marianne?' he asked her and sounded concerned.

'Oh, Harvey, I am so glad that you have come. We did not expect you. Esther was upset about Charles and she has run off and I cannot find her anywhere.'

'Goddammit, the silly girl, but I was half expecting this to happen. She has been hiding her emotions for too long. Marianne, get the stable boy to see to the carriage and the horses and then go inside and get rid of that wet shawl. I have a thick cloak in the carriage, I will put it round me and go and look for her. Have you any idea where she might be?'

'I tried the summer house and she is not there. I suppose it is possible that she could have run down to the lodge. But she will be very wet wherever she is, she went out without a shawl or a pelisse.'

'The silly girl,' he said again. 'Do as I say, Marianne, and I will go down to the lodge.'

Marianne waited a long time for him to come back and began to wonder where he was. The lodge was not far as Welford Grange had only a short drive. She stood looking out of the window and noticed that the rain was not quite so heavy as it had been. Where would I go if I wanted to be alone and out of the rain, she was asking herself. There is nowhere except the summer house and the copse . . .

The copse.

She felt a lifting of her spirits. The two of them had often walked in the copse and the trees were thick; some of the firs would give good shelter. Harvey may not have thought of it. My shawl is still wet, but I can take an old cloak. She set off quickly and half-walked, half-ran in the direction of the copse. There was no sign of Esther or of Harvey.

She started walking towards the centre and as she came in sight of the memorial, she stopped short, her heart beating fast, her breath coming quickly.

Standing beneath a tall fir tree near the memorial were Harvey and Esther. They were in each other's arms.

# 10

Earlier on, Esther on rushing out of the drawing-room, had run straight to the copse. It was a favourite place of hers and she knew that it would afford her some shelter.

Out of breath, she leaned against the memorial; the rain had soaked through her dress and she was wet to the skin. She did not notice.

Her only thought was of Charles; she had a nightmare of a vision of him mounting the guillotine in La Place de la Grève, then lying down to be no more. All these days, she had deluded herself into thinking that he was close to her, that she would never lose him completely. But the thought of having to write to her unfeeling Aunt Florence and say that Charles was dead had struck at her like a deadly weapon, as deadly as the guillotine itself.

She felt the rain flattening her hair to her head and moved without thought of moving to the shelter of a tall pine close by. She felt the dry pine needles under her feet in stark contrast to the drenching wetness of her dress.

Perhaps I will die of pneumonia, she thought, and I will be with Charles in some other place. I wonder if heaven really is a place? she found she was asking herself. It doesn't seem very probable though I have always believed in heaven. Perhaps it is just a state of mind where our souls will meet in peace, where I can meet Charles and we will be again as one . . .

So her thoughts wandered, almost as though she was already in the delirium of a fever. She lost count of time and she did not hear Harvey's first call.

'Esther, are you there?'

Then the sound of her name penetrated her ears.

'Esther, Esther.'

She opened her eyes and looked across the clearing in the copse. It was, it must be Harvey.

'Harvey, oh Harvey.'

She stayed still and he ran towards her. She was in his arms and he held her very close to him.

'You are wet through, my child, let me put this shawl around you; what are you doing here?'

She stayed in his arms and felt the comfort of putting her cheek against his already damp waistcoat. I can tell Harvey, she thought, he will understand. He cannot be for me; I am sure that Marianne loves him in spite of what she tells me.

'It is Charles,' she said at last. 'I know now that he is dead. I have to write and tell Aunt Florence that he is dead. What shall I do, Harvey, what shall I do?'

Harvey bent and kissed her cheek. 'What you are going to do, young lady, is to let me take you back to the Grange and Marianne will put you in a tub of hot water. Then I will help you write the note to your aunt and you will give it to me. Tomorrow, I am going to London, so I will seek out your aunt and tell her everything. Is all that understood?'

Esther lifted her head and looked at him. 'You are so good, Harvey. Please let me give you a kiss.' She reached up and kissed him on the lips.

It was this embrace which Marianne had seen as she entered the copse, before turning away and running swiftly home.

Harvey hurried Esther as fast as she could manage, for she was starting to shiver and he realized the urgency of the hot bath tub.

Marianne came out to meet them as they entered the Grange. 'You have found her, Harvey,' she said with no expression in her voice. She could still feel the hurt of seeing them in each other's arms.

'She was in the copse. She is wet through and shivering, Marianne; can you arrange for some hot water for her?'

'I have done so,' she replied and did not meet his eyes. 'Janey has taken hot water and the tub up to Esther's bedroom.'

She put her arms round the shivering girl. 'Let me take you upstairs, Esther, Janey will help you.'

Coming back down the stairs, she found Harvey in the drawing-room and standing close to the fire in an attempt to dry off.

'You are wet, too, Harvey, you should be on your way back to Broadoaks.'

'I must wait for Esther,' he told her.

'Why is that?'

'She is going to write a note to her aunt and I am taking it when I go to London tomorrow.' His eyes searched her face. 'What is it, Marianne? You look 'put out', I think the expression is.'

Marianne felt the truth wrenched from her. 'I saw you kissing Esther when you were in the copse; you have fallen in love with her, Harvey?'

He stared at her, then, and to her astonishment, have a loud laugh.

'You are jealous, Marianne Welford, you are jealous because Esther kissed me . . . yes, that is what it was. I told her that I would help her write the note and take it to her aunt tomorrow; she reached up and kissed me. Did it upset you, Marianne, does it mean you care for me after all?'

'Of course I care for you, I have always done so,' she said crossly. 'I just thought it too soon to try and engage Esther's affections. She was very upset at the thought of writing about Charles's death and that is why she ran out. I must thank you for going after her. You have not answered my question. Have you fallen in love with Esther?'

They were facing each other and Harvey put out his hands and grasped her by the arms. 'I have *not* fallen in love with Esther though I do feel very sorry for her. I do not allow myself thoughts of love while this wretched business with France is going on. But it somehow pleases me that you feel a little jealous — did you follow us to the copse? Is that what happened? I found her there as you know, soaking wet as much with tears as with the rain. I took her in my arms to comfort her, what else could a gentleman do? And then she kissed me and you saw it, and you were jealous. I like that, my Marianne, I like that, I vow I do.'

Marianne was becoming flushed. 'You are detestable to roast me when we are in the middle of an upset about poor Esther. I must go and see if she is recovering and I will bring her down again.'

'Not before I have had my second kiss of the morning,' he taunted her.

'What do you mean? Harvey . . . '

But Marianne's voice was silenced as Harvey took her into his arms, holding her close and kissing her until she could feel the dampness of his coat against her . . .

'Harvey, Marianne.'

Esther's voice came from the doorway. To see them kissing did not surprise her and she advanced into the drawing-room full of gratitude.

'I feel better now,' she told them. 'I am sorry I was so upset that I ran off. It was foolish when it was so wet and I thank you for coming after me.'

'I will help you write your note, Esther,' said Harvey. 'It need only be a few words, for I will take it to your aunt myself and I will explain your circumstances. From what I have heard of her from you, she will be quite pleased to see you settled at Welford Grange. You are certain that is what you wish?'

Esther smiled. 'Marianne is insistent and so is Sir Thomas. I have never met with such kindness, and you too, of course, Harvey.'

Marianne brought paper, and pen and ink and the note was soon written.

Harvey left them with a smile for each of them, a formal bow and a kiss to the hand; he said that he expected to be away for several weeks and would be with them again at Christmas time.

The two girls settled down quietly for the rest of the day and Marianne had the impression that the incident in the morning had helped Esther in coming to terms with her grief.

★   ★   ★

Harvey, for his part, was driven to London in his carriage the next morning. He spent the rest of the day attending to various parliamentary duties, being prepared to seek out Lady Peddar the following day.

He did not know her personally, but was acquainted with the sons of some of her contemporaries. The note which Esther had written was addressed to North Audley Street and as this was not far from Harvey's own fashionable London house, he decided to set off on foot to visit Lady Peddar.

He gave his card at number ten of a street of fashionable Georgian houses and thought immediately that Lady Peddar had been left in fortunate circumstances by the late Lord Peddar. It would seem that Esther had not been so fortunate.

The footman returned and conducted Harvey up the stairs to the drawing-room; he was told that Lady Peddar had not had the intention of receiving visitors, but as she had noticed that Mr Burrage-Smith was a Member of Parliament, she had thought it possible that he might be of use to her. The information mystified Harvey.

Lady Peddar, he found, was formidable. Dressed in what he thought to be grosgrain and of a deep, rich and unflattering red, she was a large, severe-looking lady and at the moment of their introduction, appeared to be somewhat disturbed.

To Harvey's surprise, she was not alone.

Sitting at a table, not far from the fireplace, was a young man of seemingly careless habit, wearing no more than a cambric shirt and stuff breeches.

'Mr Burrage-Smith, I have consented to see you because I observed from your card that you are a Member of Parliament; it may suit my purpose to be able to consult you. I have my niece's husband staying with me in unfortunate circumstances. May I introduce you to Mr Charles Bolton.'

The young man rose and gave a slight bow. 'Honoured,' he said and sat down again.

Harvey, thinking that he must be going

mad, was speechless.

Had he heard the name aright? Lady Peddar had said 'her niece's husband'. Esther? Charles?

Words, thoughts, questions teemed through his brain until he was caught up in a whirl of conjecture, possibilities, almost of fantasy. He looked around him as though it might help resolve his bewilderment and found that he was in a strange room — not large, but cluttered with sofas and easy chairs, a card table, a bureau, a bookcase. The thing which struck him most was the luxurious damask-laid wall coverings of a red not very different from Lady Peddar's dress.

He tried to think clearly: this was a room in North Audley Street; Lady Peddar sat in front of him with bulging eyes, a young man sat gloomily at the table.

'You have nothing to say, Mr Burrage-Smith?' came the boom of Lady Peddar's voice.

Harvey found his voice at last. 'Would you object to introducing the young gentleman again, Lady Peddar?'

'I will do so if you wish. He is Mr Charles Bolton and he is my niece's husband, as I said. He has been in grave trouble and has come to me searching for his wife. Unfortunately I have no idea where Esther is.'

Esther, she has said the name, Harvey thought, even more stunned. 'Esther? Your niece's name is Esther?' he shot at her.

'Yes, of course it is. Have I not had the rearing of her? I should know that her name is Esther, she is Mrs Esther Bolton.'

Harvey went crazy. He shook Lady Peddar by the hand, then went to the table and sat down by the young gentleman who was said to be Charles.

'Goddammit,' shouted Harvey, then had the sense to lower his voice. 'You cannot be Charles Bolton. He is dead. He went to the guillotine in Paris. Esther saw him go, she is distraught. Tell me, tell me the truth, damn you. Are you Charles Bolton of Forster's, late of Paris? Tell me before I go mad.'

The young gentleman shot out a hand and grasped Harvey fiercely by the arm. 'What are you saying? You tell me. Do you know Esther? Do you know where she is? Why are you here? Who are you, for God's sake, who are you?'

Harvey drew in his breath deeply. 'Let us calm down and try and answer each other's questions. Are you indeed Charles Bolton of Forster's — and why aren't you dead? We thought you were dead.'

Charles — for it was he — got up. 'Yes, I am Charles Bolton. I escaped from the tumbrel on the way to the guillotine and managed to find my way to London. But I did not know what had happened to Esther, so I came straight to Lady Peddar to see if she had received any news. I have been here for two days and I am going crazy with worry about Esther. Do you really have news of her?'

Harvey, too, had risen and tried to speak calmly. 'I have just come from her, she is in Sussex. She wanted to write to her aunt — Lady Peddar — to say where she was staying and as I was coming to London on business, I said I would bring the letter. I have it here.'

They stared at each other. 'You mean that Esther is safe? Oh, I thank you . . . oh, what can I say?'

And Harvey Burrage-Smith and Charles Bolton clasped each other round the shoulders; Charles had tears in his eyes.

'And you are alive,' said Harvey. 'It is as though you have risen from the dead. It is a miracle.'

'I think I had better see this letter to make sure that this is not all a nonsense,' interrupted Lady Peddar.

Harvey looked at her with dislike. It was little wonder that Esther had not wished to return to North Audley Street. He withdrew the letter from his pocket. 'Here it is, Lady Peddar. I was with Esther when she wrote it.'

*Dear Aunt Florence*
*I write to tell you that calamity has overtaken us. Charles has gone to the guillotine and I was rescued from Paris by Mr Harvey Burrage-Smith, the bearer of this letter.*
*He is a neighbour of Sir Thomas Welford and I am staying at Welford Grange for the time being.*
*I hope you are well*
*Esther*

'Yes, it is her writing, and no mistake,' said Lady Peddar.

'She is well, my little Esther?' asked Charles eagerly.

'She has been upset naturally, but she is bearing up very well. Sir Thomas's daughter, Marianne, is the same age as Esther and they have become good friends.' Harvey paused. 'I think we will have to be very careful how we tell her that you are still alive — she will be overjoyed and shocked at the same time.'

'Would you take me to her, Mr Burrage-Smith . . . ?'

'Please call me Harvey and I will call you Charles, we cannot be formal. Yes, certainly I will take you, but I think not until tomorrow. It is obvious that we must find clothes for you.'

'But I cannot find a tailor who would fit me in a day.'

'No, of course not,' replied Harvey. 'What I would suggest — with Lady Peddar's permission — is that we visit your tailor for a fitting this afternoon, then you can come back to my house in Hill Street. We are much of a build and I am sure that we can find some breeches and a coat and waistcoat to fit you. We will go out to dine, and after dinner, you can tell me the story of your miraculous escape and I will tell you how we managed to get Esther out of France.'

Charles Bolton had come to life; he was a good-looking young gentleman with soft brown hair and dark eyes and his looks improved even as Harvey was talking to him. The haggard, drawn look had gone from his face and he was both cheerful and hopeful.

'I cannot begin to thank you,' he said to Harvey, unaware that Esther had kept saying the same thing to her rescuers. Then he turned to Lady Peddar who was still looking at the letter. 'Lady Peddar, you will excuse me? I must go to Esther and I think we will leave her in Sussex for a little while; I have to find us a home in London and the country air will do her good.'

Lady Peddar nodded. 'I will admit to being pleased for you, Charles, and now I will not have the bother of it all. I have an engagement this afternoon and this evening, there is a loo party I wish to attend. Mr Burrage-Smith, I thank you for bringing me Esther's letter, I bid you good day.'

Outside the house, the two young gentlemen looked at each other.

'What a gorgon,' said Harvey. 'It is no wonder that Esther did not wish to go back.'

'No, her's was not a happy childhood,' agreed Charles. 'But fortunately, we met each other when Esther was only eighteen and we have had two very happy years together in Paris. In spite of all the trouble, that is; I had always thought that I was safe. I was no French aristocrat.' He looked up and down North Audley Street. 'You have your carriage here?'

'No, my house is only in Hill Street which is just the other side of Grosvenor Square, it is only a few minutes' walk. Do you object?' Harvey asked.

'Not at all, it is good to get away from Lady Peddar and I am keen to hear all about Esther,' Charles replied readily. 'I am still wondering if I am going to awake from a dream!'

'It is no dream; we will go to Hill Street for luncheon and I will try to dress you decently. Then we must find a tailor; you have a tailor in London?'

'Yes, I go to Bempton in Jermyn Street. He is very obliging and will fit me out in a very few days.'

By the time all this was accomplished, the two gentlemen felt themselves to be well acquainted and they repaired to Albemarle Street to enjoy a substantial dinner at the Clarendon Hotel.

Over dinner, they were rarely silent, but they waited until they had reached the quiet sanctuary and a bottle of port in Harvey's house in Hill Street before they related the stories of their capers through France.

The house was smaller than most in Hill Street, but Harvey found it convenient and comfortable. The drawing-room was spacious, but he had no library or study; the dining-room was no bigger than would hold a dining-table and six chairs with a handsome bow-fronted mahogany sideboard, which he had purchased new when he had moved into the house. All the other furniture was a mixture of comfort and shabbiness and had been brought from his parents' home in

Suffolk when he had needed a home in London.

By the fireplace in the drawing-room, he had placed two winged easy chairs from an earlier period; the green velour was worn, but he liked them and found them comfortable.

The fireplace itself was imposing. It was of the white marble usually found in London homes; but directly under the mantelshelf was a striking panel in a Greek key pattern, the gold of the pattern contrasting markedly with the white fireplace.

A decanter and their glasses on a small table between them, Harvey and Charles settled down to recount their experiences.

Charles was insistent on one thing. 'I will not say a word of how I escaped until I know how Esther was brought to this country.'

And so the tale was told. How Harvey had taken Marianne with him and their uncomfortable stay in the jail; how Esther had been in captivity, but relatively well treated; and finally, of their successful drive to Dieppe and their crossing to Newhaven.

Charles was silent at the end of the tale. 'You risked your lives for her, Harvey, you and Marianne. How can I ever repay you?'

'It is enough that she is safely home,' Harvey replied. 'Don't forget that I have been in and out of France many times these last years. I soon learned the pitfalls and the dangers; I learned the safe places, where we would be kindly received. It is all experience, Charles, and with luck behind us, we have succeeded. I am not the only one to bring the aristocracy of France over to England.' He paused thoughtfully. 'You must not forget that we were sometimes aided by the presence of mind of those trying to escape. Look at Esther. She had the thought and courage to go into Forster's in Paris and leave her message. Without that, we would not have known about her. You have been back to the bank?'

Charles shook his head. 'I could not go dressed as I was, and I was desperate to find Esther. It did not occur to me that she could have succeeded in sending a message through Forster's. Is she not wonderful, Harvey, as well as being very pretty? It would not surprise me to learn that you had fallen in love with her.'

Harvey grinned. 'I will admit to being very taken with her, but my heart is in another place. I will say no more, but I will tell you of the incident in the copse at Welford Grange when Marianne found Esther and me in each others arms!'

'Have I cause to be jealous?' asked Charles.

'Certainly not, she is a sweet girl and she

kissed me very nicely — it was a thank you kiss. But she is all yours and tomorrow morning, we will journey into Sussex to find her — '

Charles made an interruption. 'If you don't mind, I think I should present myself at Forster's before we go. What do you think?'

Harvey nodded. 'You are correct and we will go there first thing in the morning. But now, you have some explaining to do. I am eager to know how you succeeded in escaping the guillotine.'

'It will take all night,' said Charles.

'Never mind that. Proceed.'

# 11

It was very quiet in the drawing-room of number ten Hill Street; the only sounds which penetrated the room from the outside were the wheels of the carriages and the hoofs of the horses as they made their way down the street, taking their occupants to and from their various evening entertainments.

Inside, there came a crack or a spit from the logs burning in the grate when some hidden spot of sap was caught in a flame.

The two gentlemen were silent and Harvey could see that Charles was lost in the nightmare of the past.

'It is over now, Charles,' he said gently. 'You are in England and tomorrow you will see Esther.'

'Esther.' The word burst from him and Charles was catapulted into a scene which would never be banished from his memory. 'I did not even say goodbye to her, Harvey. There was no time, it all happened so quickly and so violently, too. The front door of our house burst open and three men stood there, I could see the tumbrel outside. Esther was crying, clinging to me and calling out my name. But the guards forced her away and one of the others said, 'Charles Bolton, your turn for Madame la Guillotine'. They dragged me off, or I should say that two of them did; the third stayed with Esther and said that he had a carriage for her — I could hear her cries. I was forced up on to the tumbrel — it is only a cart, you know, drawn by one horse — but as I got up, I could see that there was also a small carriage at the house and I guessed that they were going to take Esther somewhere. 'My wife' I called out, but the guard slapped his hand over my mouth.

'"She is being taken to a place of safety, monsieur. Our orders were Mr Bolton only for La Place de la Grève. Keep still.'

'I was struggling to be free, but he had a strong hold on me. As the shock wore off, I started to think. First of all, I looked to see where we were and recognized the long Rue St Honoré easily; I thought to myself, only the Tuileries between us and La Place de la Grève where the guillotine was doing her ghastly work.

'The road was very busy, crowded with carriages, carts, the occasional barouche and, as usual, all the heavy farm wagons going to and from the markets. Some of them were covered, some were no more than carts not

248

unlike the tumbrel and those were usually the ones with the livestock in them. Pigs, sheep, crates of poultry, even the odd cow or two.

'Drivers were shouting at each other for the carts were going in both directions, into the city and away from it; sometimes there was scarcely room to pass. But I did notice one thing and that was that the farm carts were passing so close to the tumbrel, it would be possible to jump from one to the other. But would it be possible? In the first place, the guard was holding me in an iron grip; then I thought that even if I did manage to jump into a farm cart, they would come after me . . . I am sorry, Harvey, I am taking a long time. I seem to be seeing every little detail, reliving it all.'

'Don't worry, Charles. I have seen enough of Paris in these terrible times to be able to imagine just what you are describing. Please go on.'

'I knew I had to wait for an opportunity and not far from the end of the Rue St Honoré, I saw it. Two things happened simultaneously to give me my chance and I took it. There was a block in the traffic and all was confusion; drivers were shouting and waving their arms, nothing was moving. We were stuck there and alongside us was a farm cart laden down with pigs, the poor things had hardly room to move. Our driver was swearing and cursing and shouting something to the guard. Oh, it all happened so quickly, I can hardly believe it even now; you will laugh, Harvey.'

'It is no laughing matter, Charles.'

'No, you are right. My guard loosed his hold on my arm to try and move towards the driver to hear what was being shouted at him. In that second, I wrenched my arm from him, knocked him over and I jumped into the pig cart. They squealed and they were filthy, but I didn't care. I crouched down in their midst and they seemed to move close as though they knew they had to hide me — I expect that is my imagination! I hardly dared to breathe, I could hear the guard yelling at the top of his voice; but the traffic blockage suddenly cleared, the farm cart got free of it and went trundling off down the road in the opposite direction from the tumbrel. All I could hear were the loud shouts from the tumbrel and the squealing of pigs.

'I stayed still and I knew that I could not be seen. I had no idea how far we had gone, but gradually from the sound of the traffic, I guessed that we had left the Rue St Honoré. We were going faster and, lifting my head for a second, I thought I recognized the Rue St Antoine; we would soon be at the Pont Neuf, over the river and on our way out of the city.

'Oh, Harvey, I sat back and cried then, my head against one of the warm creatures who had saved me. I had escaped the guillotine, but I could think only of Esther. My one comfort was that she had not been taken to the guillotine, but was probably being held captive somewhere, maybe even held up for a ransom. My poor little Esther; if only I had known of your bravery then and that of Marianne, too.'

'How long were you in the pig truck, Charles?' Harvey ignored the tribute to himself. It had been his duty.

'It seemed a long time. I kept having a peep out and when I saw fields instead of buildings, I knew I had escaped from Paris. I raised my head from the animals' side — they were warm, you know, that is a funny thing to remember, is it not? After a few moments, I gave a shout. We were in a quiet country lane, it was very muddy and there was no other cart to be seen. I could see the driver was an elderly man and probably poor, too. It was a cold day, but he had no coat, just a sack over his shoulders. He did not hear me so I tried to stand up and shouted again. He turned round then and saw me standing there, in the middle of his pigs; I was still dressed as a city gentleman, but I was covered with muck. I must have looked the oddest sight for he stared at me, stopped the cart and jumped down to run to me.

''Monsieur,' he said in a rough voice. 'Who are you? What are you doing hiding in my pigs? I am on my way home from the market.'

'I told him as briefly as I could, and bless the dear man, he was a simple soul but he was sympathetic. He made me jump up beside him and he drove to his farm; it was only a few miles further on.

''What are you going to do now?' he asked me.

'I told him that my first plan was to go back to my house and see if my wife was there, though I had a suspicion that she had been taken.

'He might have been a simple, honest farmer and paid his taxes like anyone else, but he was kind-hearted and he was very practical.'

'What did he suggest that you should do?' asked Harvey.

'He had it planned in a flash. I could not go back to the city dressed like that. I was not only filthy dirty, but my clothes would give me away. I was to come to his farm where I could wash myself under the pump in the yard, he would find me a shirt and breeches, and a leather jerkin — old ones of his; if they didn't fit, *n'importe*, he said. His wife would give me something to eat, even if it was only a dish of potatoes, and then he would drive me back to the outskirts of Paris. After that, I must make my own way, he told me.'

'You succeeded in getting back to your house?'

Charles nodded. 'I did not know the part of Paris in which the good farmer left me, but all I had to do was to follow the traffic. No one took any notice of me, I was only a farm labourer even if I was still wearing my Parisian boots beneath my breeches. But, Harvey, although I had escaped, I could not be cheerful; it was Esther. I could think only of Esther.'

'You will soon be with her,' Harvey reminded him.

'I know, I cannot believe it even now. But I will tell you how I got through Paris. I walked and walked until it was night-time and very cold. I had got over the river and to a part where the houses were grander; I went to the small lodge of one of them. The man took a stick to me, but the old woman there gave me some bread and said that I could sleep in the shed. So I stayed there till morning — at least I was out of the cold. I did not trouble them again, but set off as soon as it was light; I reached our house quite quickly and I thought my heart would break.'

'They had ransacked it.' Harvey's remark was more a statement than a question.

Charles nodded. 'Everything gone except the biggest pieces of furniture; all my clothes — and Esther's. No food left, the kitchen was emptied of everything, even the knives and forks had gone. I had hoped to find food, but there was nothing. I sat down and cried then for I had no idea where Esther was. My only thought was to try and make my way back to England — '

Harvey interrupted him. 'But, Charles, did you not think of going back to Forster's?'

'Yes, I did, but there were too many things against it, the main one being that I was afraid that those on the Committee of Public Safety who had condemned me to the guillotine, would be on the lookout for me.'

'So what did you do?'

'I had a good look round for something to sell, so that at least I would have money to buy food. The furniture they had left behind was useless, it was too big to move. I wandered round thinking that it was impossible, they had even taken the curtains. Then I remembered the little room upstairs which we had never used . . . ' his voice broke. 'To tell you the truth, it was to be the nursery if ever we were blessed with children. It had never been furnished, but it did have curtains and we had put two pictures on the walls — they did not seem to fit anywhere else. They were nothing; just two watercolours of Paris we happened to have, but they were quite pleasant and I thought I might get a louis a piece for them. So I took down the curtains, wrapped them round the pictures and hurried through the streets to a dealer. I knew him because I had bought odd pieces of silver from him. He did not recognize me or question me and I went away with several coins in my pocket. I was able to buy some bread.' He stopped and looked at Harvey. 'I cannot go on, you will be tired of this tale.'

Harvey shook his head. 'No, I want to hear how you got out of France. It is not midnight yet, we will have some brandy. Was it difficult, getting out of Paris?'

'I tried to work out the best way and decided to wait outside the North Gate. There was sure to be some cart or other going to Calais, I planned to try and cross from Calais to Dover. It seemed like hours waiting there, but at last luck was on my side. A wagon was allowed through the gate, it was stacked with barrels — I thought it looked like brandy — and it stopped just where I was standing. The driver obviously thought the barrels had slipped and he got down to have a look at them. I went to help him and asked where he was going. Calais, he said, and don't stop me, I have to be there before dark to meet the boat. This lot's going to England. I nearly shouted with joy, but kept quiet and held out some coins; he looked at them and asked if I wanted a lift — he wouldn't mind, he liked company. We'll use this, he said, taking the money readily, for a bite to eat on the way.

'Well, that is nearly the end. It was an easy ride and the carter was jovial. I did not tell him the truth. You would have laughed in Calais, for I joined a band of smugglers taking the brandy to England; in any other circumstances, I would have enjoyed myself. We took the barrels out to the cutter which was waiting off Calais and the other men didn't question it. Then just off Dover, a small boat came to meet us and we got the stuff ashore and loaded the pack ponies which were waiting there; the tubmen were there, too, and I took a couple of tubs along with the rest. We left them in a farmer's barn and I sheltered there till morning.'

'But, Charles, you are making it sound like a big adventure.'

Charles grinned. 'I think that bit was. What came next wasn't such fun. I walked into Dover, no baggage, no money, hungry but not tired because I'd slept in the barn. Somehow I had to get to London.'

'However did you manage to do it?'

'I found my way to the fish market, the boats were just coming in. I was taken on and stayed there three or four days, just enough to buy bread and save something to go with the carter to London. I had enough money left to stay at a low-down London inn, but at least I was able to wash there. I made a fuss of one of the maids and she rinsed out my shirt and breeches while I slept and dried them by the kitchen range for the next morning. Harvey, you will admit that I could not present myself at Lady Peddar's stinking of fish!'

They both laughed, the tale was nearly finished. 'I suppose all that time, I had been doing something and I had been hopeful. It was when I found that Lady Peddar had received no news of Esther that the black moments came. That was until you arrived, of course. How can I begin to thank you, Harvey?'

Harvey rose at last. 'You will thank me by going to bed and sleeping well, then after breakfast in the morning, we will go to Forster's and journey into Sussex.'

'Thank you, I cannot wait to see Esther, but I feel that I must be sure that my position at Forster's is still secure.'

Harvey smiled. 'You are very wise. I will take you in the carriage to the city and I will wait for you while you speak to them. I have my man, Desmond, he lodges nearby and he will drive us. We can continue to Sussex straight from Forster's.'

They both slept well, breakfasted heartily and Desmond drove them into the city.

Harvey waited and was not impatient. He was pleased at his mission and eager to see Esther and Charles together again. Of his own affairs, he thought very little.

Charles came hurrying out of Forster's with a spring in his step and joined Harvey in the waiting carriage.

'It seems like good news, Charles,' Harvey commented.

'It is. They have given me a more senior position because of my two years in Paris, and while I am fetching Esther, they will arrange to have a house ready for us. It is not far from Hill Street, Harvey, and they will hire servants for us so that we can move straight in. Not only that, they are making me an allowance so that I can go to my tailor and Esther can renew her wardrobe. They could not have been more helpful and they were so thankful that I had managed to escape and that Esther was safely in England. I did not tell them the whole of it because I knew you were waiting. How long will it take us to get to Welford Grange, Harvey?'

'It is slow going out of London, but once we are clear of the traffic, I can usually reckon on six or seven hours to Lewes. We should be there by the middle of the afternoon if we don't stop too long for luncheon.' Harvey looked thoughtful and added, 'I think we must plan what we are going to do when we arrive; this is going to be a tremendous shock to Esther. I know she will be overjoyed, but I think it will be best when we arrive at Welford Grange, if I go in first to prepare her while you wait in the carriage. Do you agree to that, Charles?'

Charles smiled. 'Yes, of course, though I feel very impatient,' he replied.

★ ★ ★

At Welford Grange, Marianne and Esther passed the time quietly after Harvey had departed. Marianne made Esther tell her about their life in Paris, and she learned much of the sad, turbulent years in that city after the storming of the Bastille.

There had been little social life for Charles and Esther, though they did attend dinners given by other members of the staff of Forster's. For herself, Esther had not grumbled at the lack of entertainment; she had Charles coming home each day, they had a comfortable home and they were happy together.

By this time in Sussex, they were well into December and had begun to make plans for Christmas, though Esther said that she did not look forward to the festivities. She received no word from Lady Peddar, but was in no doubt that Harvey had taken the letter to that lady. The fact that her aunt had not replied came as no surprise to her, though she did realize that it was early days.

On the day of the arrival of Harvey's carriage, it was cold, crisp and fine. The two girls had walked out in the morning and after luncheon, had settled by the fireside in the drawing-room with their embroidery. Sir Thomas had asked them to work tapestry pictures which could be given as Christmas gifts to Mrs Burberry and the other farmers' wives on the estate.

When they heard a carriage come to a halt at the front door, they did not stir, imagining it to be a visitor for Sir Thomas.

But when the maid admitted the visitor and they heard Harvey's voice, both of them jumped up and Marianne ran to the door.

'Harvey, whatever are you doing here? You said that you would be in London until

Christmas. Is it bad news?'

Harvey bent and kissed her cheek. 'It is very good news, my dear. Where is Esther?'

'I am here,' said, Esther, joining them at the door.

'Go and sit down,' Harvey ordered her, but kindly. 'I have some news for you and it is going to come as a shock.'

Esther sat back in the chair looking pale and anxious. 'I do not think that I can do with any more shocks,' she told him. 'Is it my aunt? Did you find her unwell?'

Harvey went on slowly. 'Your aunt is perfectly well; up to her eyes in social engagements, it seems.' He looked up at Marianne who was staring at him; she knew him well enough to understand that he needed her help and she nodded.

Harvey took Esther's hands in his. 'Esther, listen carefully. It is Charles . . . '

'Charles . . . ?' she whispered.

'Charles is alive, Esther, he escaped from Paris and is back in England.'

'Charles . . . ' Again the whispered name, barely audible. 'Alive . . . ?' And with these words on her lips, she went into a swoon.

Marianne was there to hold the stricken girl and Harvey found the hartshorn. 'Marianne,' he said urgently. 'I have Charles in the carriage at the door, I will go and fetch him and we will leave the two of them together. Then I can tell you what has happened.'

Marianne nodded and Harvey hurried from the room. He found Charles waiting to jump from the carriage. 'Hurry, Charles. I tried to tell Esther quietly, but she has gone into a swoon. Marianne is with her.'

Charles was in the house in seconds and Harvey took him into the drawing-room.

'Oh, my dear one . . .' he gasped and he knelt down and took Esther from Marianne and held her close in his arms.

'Esther, speak to me. It is Charles. I am alive, please speak to me, Esther, *ma chérie*.'

Esther opened her eyes at the sound of his voice. 'Charles . . . oh Charles, it really is you,' she cried out.

Harvey and Marianne crept from the room.

Esther thought that she was dreaming, nothing seemed real. How could this be Charles when Charles was dead?

'I think it is a dream,' she said.

Charles acted then. He made Esther take a sip of the hartshorn, then picked her up and carried her to the sofa so that he could sit beside her and hold her in his arms.

'Esther,' he said softly. 'Don't you know me?'

She opened her eyes, searching his face, recognizing the familiar features and finally, burying her head against him.

'I cannot believe it,' came the muffled tones. 'How can it be?' She lifted her head, put up a hand then traced her fingers over his features as though the feel of him might be more convincing than the sight had been. 'It really is you,' she said again. 'How can it be? I thought you had gone to the guillotine, that you were dead.'

'I managed to escape, *ma petite*. It is a long, long story which I have told to Harvey. I will tell you later when your good friend, Marianne, is with us.'

'Charles, I am beginning to believe it even if I do not understand. How did you know that I was here?' she asked him.

'I went straight to your aunt when I arrived in England, but she had heard nothing. I feared for you, Esther, for I knew that you had been taken from our house. Then Harvey came to Lady Peddar with your note and . . . oh, the joy of it. To know that you were safe here in England. I came as soon as I could, I am sorry if I gave you a shock.'

Esther was looking at him. 'You look thin, Charles, were you ill?'

He shook his head. 'No, not ill, just hungry.

I lived on little more than bread for many days.'

'Charles, we must tell Marianne. Did Harvey tell you that she came into France to look for me, she pretended to be his wife. She is so good, you must meet her.'

'Let me give you a kiss and I will go and look for them,' he said happily.

The kiss was sweetly and briefly exchanged, Charles went off and came back with Marianne, Harvey and Sir Thomas.

Charles was properly introduced to Marianne and he took her hand and kissed her cheek. 'I will never be able to thank you sufficiently,' he told her.

Dinner took a long time at Welford Grange that day; the tales were told amidst laughter — the pigs and the fish at Dover — and tears for Paris itself.

Harvey insisted that he must return to London the next day and it was decided that Esther and Charles should go with him. They promised to purchase a carriage and return to Welford Grange for Christmas.

Marianne saw Harvey off and found him in a sombre mood. 'You have done so much for them, Harvey. If only it could be an end to all the trouble in France.'

'I fear that it is only a beginning, Marianne.'

'What do you mean?' she asked sharply.

'I cannot speak of it now, but I will be back before Christmas and perhaps I will have more to tell you then. Goodbye, my dear Marianne. May I kiss you?'

She smiled and lifted her face, thinking that this was a very polite Harvey. His lips touched hers and he was gone.

The next day, he called at the Grange for Esther and Charles, and Marianne waved them goodbye.

There followed a lonely time for Marianne. A letter from Lucy asked her father's permission to spend Christmas with the de Charnay family in London. Another letter from Esther told of her new home and the joy of being with Charles again. Nothing was heard from Harvey, and Marianne imagined him to be busy with affairs of state.

The week of Christmas brought a radiant Esther and a contented Charles who was once again installed at Forster's.

But by Christmas Eve, there was still no sign of Harvey and Marianne felt both worried and miserable. She was glad to have Esther to talk to; by this time, Esther knew the state of Marianne's heart even if Marianne herself was not sure of her feelings for Harvey.

'I am sure that Harvey cares for you,

Marianne,' said Esther on Christmas Eve. They were sitting by the fire together, Charles having gone shooting with Sir Thomas.

Marianne ignored Esther's words and smiled at her friend. 'I thought he was falling in love with you at one time,' she said.

Esther laughed. 'It was just his way of being kind to me when I was missing Charles so badly. He will come galloping over from Broadoaks tomorrow morning to wish you a happy Christmas and to ask you to marry him.'

But Marianne shook her head and kept her thoughts to herself.

Christmas dinner was eaten at midday and by early afternoon, Marianne could bear it no longer. She must find out what had happened to Harvey. They would have news at Broadoaks.

It was easy enough to leave Esther and Charles together and Marianne put on her warmest riding dress, mounted Kirsty, her mare, and went over to Broadoaks at a gallop.

She arrived just as Desmond and the carriage was stopping at the front door. Harvey has been visiting elsewhere, she told herself, and felt both neglected and angry.

She jumped down from Kirsty and went up to the carriage to greet Harvey as he stepped out.

Then her breath was taken away from her.

The door of the carriage was opened and out stepped Mme Bézier.

'Mme Bézier . . . ' gasped Marianne, then realizing what she had said, corrected herself. 'Harvey.'

Then Harvey had the audacity to speak in Mme Bézier's voice and in French. '*Ma chérie*, you are here to meet me. How very nice of you. Now I can ask you to marry me.'

Marianne flew at him and he took her hands.

'Harvey Burrage-Smith, what does it mean? Why are you Mme Bézier again? Where have you been all this time? And what do you mean by asking me to marry you in such a ridiculous fashion? *Nom de Dieu*, take off that absurd bonnet.'

'Marianne, my dearest girl, we cannot stop here talking at the steps of the carriage. Take Kirsty to the stalls and join me in the drawing-room.'

Marianne flew to do his bidding and found him — still in his black clothes — warming himself by the fire.

'I will give *you* the pleasure of taking my bonnet off,' he said to her and there was a teasing chuckle in his voice.

Marianne undid the strings and lifted the flopping, brimmed bonnet, which hid his face so successfully, from his head.

'There you are,' she said. 'Harvey, you look tired. What is it all about?'

'Marianne, I will wish you a happy Christmas, then I will order tea for you; while you are drinking it, I will go and get rid of Mme Bézier for ever.'

Marianne watched him hurry out of the room and did not know whether to laugh or cry. She loved Harvey. She had known it all along, but had tried to keep the love hidden from herself. But when she had taken off the bonnet and there was *her* Harvey, she knew that she loved him. He had jokingly asked her to marry him and once upon a time, they had been formally betrothed, but she had no idea of his feelings for her. Would she know any more when he returned as Mr Harvey Burrage-Smith?

She was astonished at how quick he was. It seemed only minutes before he was at her side, dressed handsomely in deep blue coat over cream breeches and waistcoat; his neck cloth looking as though he had spent all day arranging it.

'You do look different,' she exclaimed, 'and here I am in my riding dress.'

'I like you in your riding dress, it fits you to perfection and it looks like the Marianne Welford I have always known and loved.'

Marianne gazed at him. 'What did you say?'

'Something about the girl I have always known and loved,' he repeated evenly and showing no emotion.

'You never said so before; you have never told me that you loved me even when we were betrothed.'

'I could not tell you that I loved you then, I could not allow myself to say it, not until this very moment.'

'Why?' she demanded and thought that she sounded quite rude.

'You know of all my missions into France. They were too dangerous, I might not have returned.'

'And now they are over?' The question came hopefully.

They were standing very close together and he looked down at her with a smile. 'They are over, Marianne Welford, and I can tell you that I love you and ask you to marry me — and, Marianne, do you think that I could undo a few of the buttons of your riding dress so that I can see the little bit of you underneath all that warm green kerseymere?'

'Sir.' The single word was a protest, for his fingers had quickly undone the buttons at the neck and his lips were on the pale skin of her breasts.

Marianne felt a rush of passion such as she had never felt before and she hid her face against him.

He gave a laugh. 'Have I shocked you, little one? I would like to see the whole of you, but now is not the time. We will save that pleasure.'

Marianne found words at last. 'What has happened to you? Harvey, you are not behaving as a gentleman should; not only that, why were you Mme Bézier again and why do you seem so sure it is the last time?'

'What a lot of questions. Drink your tea while I pour myself some brandy. I feel in the need of it.'

They sat facing each other across the blaze of the fire, but they were very close.

'I don't quite know where to start, Marianne. In the first place, I had hoped to ask you to marry me so that we could celebrate at Christmas time. But when I took Charles and Esther to London, instead of being told that all our efforts at bringing the émigrés over were finished, I was asked to go on one last trip. I am not going to go into details about it, except to say that I decided to risk the Mme Bézier disguise one more time. I was foolish, it nearly cost me my life, but this morning, we arrived safely back in Newhaven and I saw my charges safely on their way. An old marquis and his wife; I felt sorry for them, but they will be safely in London with their family by now. You know what happened then? You got here before me and I had not changed out of my disguise.'

'Was Desmond driving you?'

'Yes, he was, he goes with me everywhere. Did you not recognize M. Bézier?'

Marianne shook her head. 'No, I could only see the bonnet!' She was silent.

'What is it, my dear one?' he asked gently.

'How can you be sure that there will not be another time, Harvey?'

He looked at the girl he loved and knew that she would understand. 'There are changes taking place in France and on 15 December, the siege of Toulon ended. We have held the post all these months, but now it belongs to France again. The French army has a new commander; the Duke of York is losing in Flanders; the two countries are at war.' He paused and looked at her again; he saw the look of concentration on her face. 'The Revolution is taking a new turn and I think that France will change; Robespierre and Danton are already under threat and I think their end will come before the spring. We will have to hope for a better France, even if she is our enemy.'

He smiled. 'So, my sweet, here I am, Mr

Harvey Burrage-Smith MP; a modest house in London, a small estate in Sussex. No longer an adventurer, but a very dull Englishman who offers his hand and heart to Miss Marianne Welford. Do you think she might accept?'

Marianne put out a hand and he took it. 'Miss Marianne Welford is very pleased to accept, sir.'

'And the rest?' he asked jokingly.

'The rest?'

'Yes, do you love Mr Burrage-Smith, my dear?'

Marianne laughed. 'I think I have loved you for a long time, Harvey, but I would not admit to it because I was not sure if you loved me.'

'And I have always loved you, but did not dare to tell you. What shall we do to celebrate our love?'

'Shall we burn Mme Bézier's bonnet?'

Harvey laughed and laughed and Marianne thought he sounded happy. 'What a splendid idea, I will go and fetch it.'

They watched the notorious bonnet burn.

'Farewell Mme Bézier, welcome Mrs Burrage-Smith,' said Harvey.

'Not quite yet, Harvey,' replied Marianne with a smile.

'We could forego the ceremony; shall we

just creep upstairs? No one would know.'

'Harvey!'

'What is wrong with that? We love each other.'

Marianne rose from the chair and fastened the buttons of her riding dress, 'We will wait,' she said primly, but could feel the temptation and naughtiness of the moment. 'We will go and see Papa, and Charles and Esther, who will be wondering where I am. We will tell them that you are safely home and you can ask Papa if he will allow me to be your wife.'

'Rogue. Come here and let me kiss you again.'

## THE END